■ **Amalie Skram** was born Amalie Alver in Bergen, Norway, in 1846.

Brought up within a conventional middle-class environment, at seventeen she married a sea captain and accompanied him round the world. After thirteen years of marriage, she divorced her husband and it was then she started writing; *Constance Ring* was published in 1885, although by this time she had remarried. Other books include *The People from Hellemyr*, a family trilogy spanning four generations, and *Dr Hieronimus*, the story of her attempts to seek psychiatric help over the conflicting demands of being mother, wife and writer; her second husband had committed her to an asylum, believing her insane, although she was later released.

Amalie Skram died in Copenhagen in 1905.

■ *Aileen Hennes* was born in Bergen in 1953. She left Norway at sixteen and has been living mainly in Britain since. She has pursued an erratic education, mainly in fine arts.

BETRAYED

Amalie Skram

Translated by Aileen Hennes

London and New York

First published in 1892 by Pat Gyldendal, Forradt
This translation published in 1986 by Pandora Press
Routledge & Kegan Paul Ltd
11 New Fetter Lane, London EC4P 4EE

Published in the USA by
Routledge & Kegan Paul Inc.
in association with Methuen Inc.
29 West 35th Street, New York, NY 10001

Set in Sabon 10/12pt.
by Columns of Reading
and printed in the British Isles
by The Guernsey Press Co. Ltd
Guernsey, Channel Islands

Library of Congress Cataloging in Publication Data

Skram, Amalie, 1846-1905.
Betrayed.

Translation of: Forradt.
I. Title.
PT8928.F67E5   1986   839.8'236   86-12341

British Library CIP Data also available

ISBN 0-86358-114-5 (c)
     0-86358-099-8 (pb)

TRANSLATOR'S NOTES AND ACKNOWLEDGMENTS

The Norwegian language has sadly undergone continual and dramatic changes over the last seventy years, making the writings of Amalie Skram and her contemporaries sound 'quaint' to our ears and presenting a serious barrier to a lasting familiarity with these writers. To find something equally remote from present-day English one would probably have to go back to the Georgian period. I have, however, chosen to give the translation a scent of the Victorian age in which it was written (1892). For this I have had the invaluable help of Christine and John Naumann who have guided and advised me chapter by chapter.

Sometimes I have chosen to let a Norwegian flavour dominate even where it may sound strange to the British ear. This is mainly done where titles are concerned as I think it describes a basic cultural difference. 'Riber' is Captain Carl Adolph Riber, but known by friends and his wife as 'Riber'. Only his mother and their old maid, Ane, call him by his Christian name, Adolph. He is offended when a servant in his parents-in-law's household calls him familiarly 'Riber' – she should have called him Captain Riber. Although it is usual for married women to refer to their husbands by their surname it is not good bed manners and Riber hopes and pleads with Ory to grant him the sign of affection it would be to call him by his Christian name.

Another instance where the same sort of thing presented me with a choice is with the officers aboard the *Orion*. I have let them be referred to as 'mate' and 'second mate' and only on a couple of occasions where I have wanted to denote irony used the title of Mr Mate, which I believe is how they would always have been titled aboard a British ship.

In chapter two we meet Riber's mother who is referred to by Ory as 'grandma' Riber; this is not another 'foreign idiosyncrasy', but probably a device Amalie Skram used to accentuate the childishness of her heroine.

In chapter three Ory compares the noise of a London street with the event of a fire 'at home'. I feel this can do with an explanation as all Norwegians would immediately know that she was referring to the horrendous fires Bergen has suffered and still does, although to a much lesser extent nowadays. The whole town has burnt down twice in its history. It consists mainly of small wooden houses and narrow alleyways and is frequently invaded by strong sea winds which can whip a fire up dangerously. I would think all Bergen citizens remember at one time or another being woken at night by firemen asking them to evacuate just in case a fire in the neighbourhood should suddenly change direction. The blaze, roar, commotion and sometimes panic obviously leaves a strong impression.

Last but not least I thank my husband, Ole Bendik Madsø, who has wanted to see Amalie Skram's work in translation as much as myself and has assisted me all along, finding all the Biblical quotations, all the nautical expressions, frequently reading out a dialogue aloud, that I might better judge its dramatic effect, and who has also written the foreword.

FOREWORD

The short span of consecutive Norwegian literary history, dating back only to the 1840s, presents us with a group of writers, who, however different they may be, are similar in the respect that they are much more at ease in the climate of modern European literature than one might have expected from writers for so long isolated from the cultural mainstream of Europe. At the time Amalie Skram lived (1846 to 1905) this characteristic is particularly striking when one considers that Norway had been under foreign rule for more than 400 years and had been kept in a state of subservience. The political unrest that characterized Europe in the nineteenth century also spread to Norway and caused a reawakening of patriotic feelings which eventually led to independence in 1905. The search for national identity as well as the creation of national institutions gave rise to a need for better educated people.

The lack of educational facilities at home drove large numbers of young artists and intellectuals abroad to the academic and artistic centres of France and Germany. Trading people went to Britain and Norwegian seamen travelled all over the world. They returned with a desire for changes, but in the country as a whole there was the general feeling that in re-establishing national identity one should aim at a balance between traditional values and modern trends within politics, science and the arts. This sometimes led to astonishing paradoxes or compromises, probably best illustrated by a few examples:

Bjørnstjerne Bjørnson, writer (Nobel prizewinner), orator and agitator whose personality and ideas came to dominate the period, personified this mixture of traditional and new values. He untiringly reminded the nation of its 'great past' yet at the same time he was an enthusiastic spokesman for modern technology. His sympathy for the poor and deprived did not prevent him from advocating an almost Calvinistic morality of personal responsibility; a blatant male chauvinist, he was the founder of the Norwegian Women's Liberation Movement and though at times an outspoken disbeliever, author of some of the nation's most beautiful hymns.

These are all paradoxes that reflect lasting national characteristics and are typical examples of how the writers of the time not only represented but actually came to create attitudes and idiosyncrasies that were to shape the nation in the years to come.

Amalie Skram (born Amalie Alver, Bergen, 1846) is another example of how the artists of the period came to influence society not only through their writing but also through their behaviour. By being 'just a woman', she never had the opportunity of studying, either at home or abroad. She nevertheless came to see more of the world than did most of her contemporaries. By being married off to a Danish sea captain at the age of seventeen and accompanying him aboard his ship for the following thirteen years, she had ample opportunity both to observe and to study.

Though her writing shows easily detectable foreign influences (mainly French), she remains Norwegian – almost in the same overt sense that the great Russian writers are first and foremost Russians. This comparison is not an incidental one for she is the only Scandinavian writer who is frequently compared to the Russians.

Her marriage was not a happy one, however; after those thirteen years she had spent at sea (during which time she had two sons) the marriage broke up and left her struggling to make ends meet and fighting for the custody of her children. By that time she had moved to Christiania (Oslo) where she made her first hesitant steps towards the literary career she was soon afterwards to pursue as a full-time occupation.

Though her life so far would seem to have provided ample background for the Exotic Tale, she chose from the start to treat much more explosive material – mainly the relationship between husband and wife, whilst her experiences from abroad played only an incidental part.

The husband/wife theme was to occupy her for the next seven years and resulted in four novels and a great number of short stories. *Betrayed* (1892) was the fourth and final one in the sequence and also the most autobiographical one. After that she went on to complete her great epic from the west coast of Norway, *The People from Hellemyr*, which she had started between her marriage novels. This undertaking was to earn her a position as a major writer, but also caused her to have a mental breakdown and ruined her health for the rest of her life.

Early on in her writing career she had remarried – this time to a Danish author, Erik Skram, a man rare at the time in that he encouraged her in her struggle for artistic and personal freedom. She nevertheless found it difficult to combine the functions of mother and artist. Even more so when she had a girl with Skram in the middle of her work on *The People from Hellemyr* and she had to leave her home periodically to get the solitude in which she needed to write. It made her feel guilty and gave her a sense of failure in addition to the nervous tension her work produced in her. The situation was not made easier by the disapproval of society, and she was approaching a nervous breakdown when her husband intervened and suggested she seek help from the prominent Danish psychiatrist Knud Pontoppidan. She consented to spend a week or two at his hospital; once there, she found herself declared insane (a diagnosis solely based on conversations the doctor had had with her husband), and was detained against her will. In this Pontoppidan apparently had the consent of her husband who never came to see her, even after she had managed to smuggle a note to him in which she implored him to come and see her. Either he must have wanted her out of the way or he was simply so impressed by the doctor's authority that he made no objection to his decisions.

After a while she was transferred to another hospital for the incurably insane, but the head doctor there soon released her as he found no evidence of the alleged insanity. By then she was in a state of utter mental and physical exhaustion, and as she did not want to see her husband again, lived the remaining years of her life with her daughter.

However diminished she felt at her release from hospital, before finishing the last volume of *The People from Hellemyr*, she wrote a two-volume novel about her experiences in the psychiatric ward (*Professor Hieronimus* and *At St. Jørgen*), which led to Dr Pontoppidan having to resign as head of the hospital in Copenhagen (in spite of strong support from colleagues). However, Amalie Skram never recovered from the experience of confinement and she died in 1905 at the age of fifty-nine.

At the time of her death Norway was rejoicing in its newly-gained independence and had no time for pessimistic messages, fully developed in her last novels. The school of Naturalism, to which she adhered (apparently by choice as well as by inclination), lends itself better to exposing or fighting the evils of this world than to expressing hope and exuberance in life. Even her friends, including Bjørnson, thought her writing obscene, gloomy and sordid, and tried in vain to persuade her to join in the chorus of more fashionable literary tunes.

Amalie Skram is the first writer in Norway to have dealt in a direct way with the subject of sexuality – a subject not easily dealt with in Norway, partly because of the prevailing puritan tendency. Though she did not suffer the fate of many contemporary and later artists, who had their works banned, the reaction to Amalie Skram's marriage novels was one of disgust and remained so until recently.

The characters she portrays have an expressive directness which may sound coarse at times to the British ear. It would, however, be wrong to interpret them as less inhibited than, for instance, their British contemporaries, who would tend to express their emotions less emphatically. One should remember that the Norwegian nation was still basically a rural one; middle-class society (however much it resented it) was for a long time to rub shoulders with the peasants, even in the midst of their own families. Middle-class characteristics blended strangely with the unsophisticated directness or even naïvety – still dominant in the population.

Ory, the heroine of *Betrayed* is as typical of this as are any of the other characters, and it is the mixture of almost brutal directness and naive belief in acquired middle-class illusions that makes her such a forceful influence. Without her directness she would have appeared as priggish and lacrimose as some early Victorian heroines. Her forcefulness, however, puts her in a long tradition of other strong women in Norwegian literature, real or fictional, who have through the centuries themselves committed, or exorted their men to commit, acts of bravery or destruction.

Ory, when we first meet her, is a newly-wed girl of seventeen, about to set out on a voyage with her husband, a well-known sea captain, Carl Adolph Riber, who is fifteen years her senior.

Whereas Riber is a man full of authority and worldly experience, Ory herself enters marriage straight from the 'nursery', unaware of the simplest facts of life, without even the knowledge that she is expected to sleep with her husband. Confronted with this, as well as with the ways he had got his sexual experience before marriage, she takes exception to his sexuality, past and present, and becomes a mighty opponent who finally forces him to commit suicide. The expression 'mighty opponent' is not an incidental one; it is striking the way Amalie Skram in *Betrayed* draws her characters on a larger-than-life scale, even using mythological names: Ory, short for Aurora – the goddess of dawn – and Orion – the night-hunter. (It may be argued that by this she goes beyond naturalism.) Riber, the captain of the *Orion*, is a man of such extreme vigour and vitality that he can easily be compared to the heroes of the Greek myths or the Norse sagas. His 'Achilles' heel' is his inability to reconcile the pure romanticism of the Victorian age (represented by Ory), almost a religion in itself as it approaches ecstasy, with his former life (the night-hunter), a life which, though tacitly accepted by society was, if exposed, still considered immoral.

Though he is encouraged by Ory to admit to the evil of his former life, it is difficult to tell to what extent Riber has any real understanding of the double standards by which he has been living. In her role as goddess and judge she is assisted by his feeling of male self-contempt (the 'Slomen') and his feeling of emptiness (his Death Wish) which makes him prostrate himself before her in order to receive her accusations.

By worshipping this young and innocent girl with self-effacing devotion, he believes he will achieve absolution as well as regain his joy in life. It never seems to occur to him that the qualities he worships in her will be gone once he has achieved the fulfilment of his desires. She will then be left as useless for the maintenance of his happiness as the women he has already enjoyed and discarded.

Neither of them is able to bridge the gap of unfilfilled expectations that develops between them. Both are living in a world of make-believe, worshipping ideals or virtues real to them only through social convention.

If Ory had loved him she might have been able to help him, even if not in the way he expected. But she remains as remote and uncompromising as Amalie Skram found the religion in which she had been brought up.

When the *Orion*, by then with a mere figurehead of a skipper, is becalmed in the doldrums, it signifies the state of battle between them. There seems to be only one solution to the stalemate. To put it in terms of myth: they will have to present the gods with a sacrifice before the ship will be allowed to proceed: either Male or Female sexuality will have to be sacrificed.

Riber has for a long time contemplated the idea of sacrificing himself for Ory. He makes a last and desperate attempt to sacrifice a scapegoat (the First Mate), but when that fails there is no solution left but for him to jump overboard.

Without wishing to overemphasize this theme, I think it is essential to the understanding of the story to see interwoven in the naturalistic pattern an allegorical picture of the eternal struggle between male and female sexuality.

One might argue that the death of Riber leaves Ory to reflect; that his sacrifice provides her with an opportunity to go beyond the limitations imposed upon her by society. This is a view that should be explored, but only in conjunction with a less optimistic view does it help to resolve the disturbing ambiguity conveyed by the novel as a whole.

This other and less optimistic view may be presented as one advocating a basic dichotomy between male and female sexuality, where the one has to die that the other might live, unless one or both are able to redefine themselves.

There is little evidence that Amalie Skram thought that possible, even when considering only this novel. It may be argued that the other novels are even more pessimistic. The feeling of impending doom throughout the novel, the use of images inspired from myth, premonitions, ghosts and dramatic weather, all seem to indicate that what happens in the novel goes beyond ordinary human predicaments stemming from transitory social conditions.

The confrontation that takes place reflects a universal struggle between opposing forces. The death of Riber may in this sense be seen as a cathartic sacrifice.

Arles, 4 February 1986
Ole Bendik Madsø

· 1 ·

'Now, Riber, have you finished yet?' Ingstad was asking his son-in-law, Captain Riber, a large man dressed for his wedding. With his blond beard, his kindly, somewhat slanting eyes and broad ivory-white forehead, he had a rather Russian appearance.

Riber unfastened his napkin, which was tucked underneath his white tie and draped down across his protruding shirt front all the way to his knees. He threw it on the table, at which all the male guests had been standing, enjoying the abundant supper of cold delicacies spread out before them. He started prowling round the dining-room, peeping through to the adjoining rooms, where tea and cakes were served for the ladies.

Ingstad followed him with his eyes. He sensed that his son-in-law was in a bad mood. He put down his fork and plate and went over to where Riber stood leaning against the dresser in the corner.

'Where has Aurora gone?' asked Riber, squinting with displeasure.

'She is probably saying goodbye to the maids and the little ones,' Ingstad answered in a friendly manner, clasping his hands behind his back while rocking to and fro on his feet in a slow rolling motion in front of Riber. He held his greying head erect and slightly drawn back as he looked about him with his bright eyes and kindly expression.

'Tell me, is Aurora at all moody or capricious?'

1

'No . . . but my dear Riber, whatever makes you think so?'

'Oh, something my mother always said,' mumbled Riber, pushing out his chest and belly, making his body arch from the broad shoulders down. 'Best to know each other for seven years and then marry if you haven't lost the urge.'

'No parents anywhere could have wished for a better child than Aurora has been,' said Ingstad gently. 'But you have to remember how young she is, barely seventeen-and-a-half, and she is now about to leave her home for good.'

He paused a moment, but as Riber just stood there and grunted, he continued half in jest: 'Be patient with her, Riber, if difficulties should arise. It can't be easy, you know, to be going on an expedition with an old seadog like yourself. Poor little thing.'

'Am I going to have a lecture from you as well!' Riber blurted out. 'I have heard nothing else the entire day, since we were sitting down and all the uncles and various friends of the family started bantering and coming out with their speeches. What did they think they were doing, the buffoons? Aurora must have got the impression that she was being handed over to the executioner.'

'But, you said in your own speech . . .' attempted Ingstad.

'Well, what the devil is one to say in those speeches which are a lot of rubbish anyway! Especially just after going to church and listening to the priest's twaddle. All the same,' continued Riber with mounting vexation, 'it might have been left at that. I was an ass not to realize that it would open the floodgates.'

'It hurts me that you've been caused offence, Riber.'

'I thought a wedding was supposed to be a celebration,' said Riber in a sulky although subdued voice, 'not a wake.'

'And then that uncle Pitter, buzzing round me like a fly and pestering me with his great hopes and drunken sentiments,' continued Riber. 'Make sure he's kept out of my way for the remainder of the evening, otherwise I'll twist his nose until the tip of it turns upwards. Christ, what a nose!' he added with disgust. 'He talks as much with that as he does with his mouth.'

'Oh, uncle Pitter, poor dear, he's very old.'

'Yes, that's it!' Riber laughed derisively. 'One too old – the other too young. Tell me, please, into which age bracket do you put that harridan of a housekeeper that, in your wisdom, you placed just opposite me at the table? – "Yes, Riber, oh, yes," Riber mockingly affected a thin, lisping voice, "please, take care of our treasure," – and every time she would stretch her scraggy arm across the table at me and go on, with no letting up, until I clinked glasses with her. In the end I refused and told her in a rather loud voice to "shut up". Then on top of this to be called "Riber" by the old hag! In heaven's name, I could never bring myself to be so familiar!'

'So, that's the reason she was being led away in floods of tears,' said Ingstad with concern. 'You might have considered the fact that she's been with us all the time we have been married and – '

'Oh! "Consider this and consider that." At sea, we never pay any attention to such trifles.'

Ingstad shook his head, his expression wavering between doubt and amusement.

'Well, I'm damned!' exclaimed Riber with renewed excitement. 'Here comes uncle Pitter. I'll pull his nose off at once – and be done with it.'

'Very well,' said a high-pitched voice in English and uncle Pitter, tall, raw-boned and crooked, with a brown wig and a clean shaven face stood in front of them. 'My dear Riber, do think carefully about all the things I have told you,' he nodded and his red nose bobbed up and down, 'yes, everything I have told you.'

Riber snorted and jerked his hand out of his pocket.

'Think of Aurora, dear Riber,' whispered Ingstad. 'It would upset her terribly.'

Riber's nostrils went white, his eyes blinked and the corners of his mouth trembled. 'If only he hadn't had that nose,' he muttered and withdrew his hand.

'I beg your pardon?' Uncle Pitter turned a rigid gaze from the one to the other.

'All right,' said Riber and shuffled his feet.

'Thank you, my honourable next of kin,' said uncle Pitter, putting both arms round Riber's neck. 'If I had had a daughter I would have let you have her. Confound it! I swear I would.'

Riber struggled to get free of the arms that were still holding him.

'. . . with confidence and a clear conscience,' uncle Pitter drivelled on. 'You are a good sort. Though heaven help us you're a bit unruly,' he said, threatening Riber with his index finger behind his neck, '. . . even brutal.'

'Let go of me now,' said Riber simply. 'Miss Thorsen is sitting over there by the door and I should very much like to talk to her.' He managed to free himself from uncle Pitter and walked towards the housekeeper.

When Miss Thorsen saw Riber advance she lifted herself hastily from her seat.

'Please, remain seated, madam,' said Riber cheerfully.

She sank back into the chair and looked timidly at him.

'It pleases me to see you are better, after being taken ill at the table.'

Miss Thorsen turned her yellow face aside and shut her toothless mouth firmly.

'I hope you are feeling much better now,' continued Riber ingratiatingly.

'Hmf, I shouldn't let it worry you, Riber,' she lisped sullenly. 'And, anyway, how is a dethent person thuppposed to feel after behaviour like yourth . . . ? It is a wonder I did not have cunvulthions.'

As Riber watched her toothless, damp mouth, he suddenly felt sick. His hands seemed to fly up of their own accord and without really knowing what he was doing, he grabbed hold of her bun and crushed it between his fingers.

Miss Thorsen raised both her hands to her head and screamed hoarsely: 'Let me be, you coarse fellow! If you are not the Evil One himthelf, you are thertainly one of Hith helperth here on earth.'

Riber laughed with relish. He turned round. Apart from uncle Pitter, who was standing by the window and unconcernedly stirring his drink, everybody had left.

'Listen,' he turned to face Miss Thorsen, who, crouching in terror, still held onto her hair with both hands, while her cat-like eyes glinted with hatred. 'I have come to make it up with you. You are a treasure, Miss Thorsen; that is what all the Ingstads say, and I would like to believe it. But the thing is, I forgot to bring back home with me the gift I'd planned to give you. The irritation over that, has caused me, twice – ahem – shall we say: to be a little rude towards you?'

'I have alwath been a rethpectable perthon,' Miss Thorsen suddenly broke into sobs 'ever thince I was young and even more tho, now that I'm getting old. That is why I think that a young bridegroom like you, should show one thome rethpect, even though one ith only common.'

'Yes – well – yes! I quite agree ma'am.' Riber strove hard to maintain his pleasant manner. 'I would like to ask a favour of you. I wonder if you would share out this money amongst the maids and others that have had so much work to do in arranging the wedding.' He brought a ten-specie note out of his waistcoat pocket. 'Will you do me that favour, Miss Thorsen?'

She grabbed the note and muttered something incomprehensible.

'And this is for you,' continued Riber. 'It is two English gold pieces which you can ask Ingstad to exchange for you at his bank. I want you to have them because I forgot to bring you the present. Please, receive them in the same good spirit as they are given.'

Miss Thorsen rose and received the money with a curtsey.

'You are at heart a generous man, Riber. That ith what I've always thaid and I will go on thaying it till the day I die, if ever I should hear anyone talk ill of. you.'

'Very good, madam. Do we part as friends then?'

'Oh, God bleth you, Riber!' Miss Thorsen gave him her bony, shrivelled hand. 'I never bear grudges, I always think of what the Good Book thays: Judge not, that ye not be judged!'

Just then, Mrs Ingstad came into the room, a brown-haired woman, dressed in silk. Riber approached her hurriedly.

'Is Aurora ready?'

'Nearly, Riber. It is a bit strange for her. She is very attached to her home and the other children. I shall go at once and ask her to hurry up.'

Mrs Ingstad left the dining-room, crossed a long, dimly-lit corridor and entered the nursery. A nightlight shone softly over four small beds and Aurora, a slim and shapely figure, stood in the middle of the floor in her white wedding dress. The long train made her appear taller than she was. She had pulled the veil away from her pale face, where two large, solemn, blue eyes contrasted strangely with the childish roundness of her cheeks.

'Now then, Aurora dear,' Mrs Ingstad touched her shoulder lightly.

Aurora threw her arms about her mother's neck and started to cry.

'Don't cry, Aurora.'

'Why don't you call me Ory, as usual,' she had to force the words out through the painful weeping. 'Oh, it is his idea! I don't want to be called anything but Ory, mummy, do you hear!'

'Yes, my dear Ory, but let's go now.'

'I'm not going to go with him! I won't, mummy.'

'Are you out of your mind, child?' Mrs Ingstad grabbed her daughter by the arms and tried to hold her back far enough to be able to look into her eyes.

'I won't go, I won't go,' sobbed Ory and clung to her mother.

'A bride who loves her husband, is about to experience the deepest joy life can offer. And you have taken him willingly and out of love, haven't you, Ory?'

'Yes, but now I'm going to sleep in the same bed as him,' – her voice fell to a faint and anguished whisper as she straightened herself up and walked quickly across the room. Then, leaning against a chest of drawers, she turned to face her mother. 'Grandma Riber has told me that she has brought her own mother's bridal bed down from the attic for me to have,' she took a deep breath and looked at her mother with an expression as though she expected her to faint from the horror of it.

'You have known all along!' Ory's neck grew tense. 'You have known and never said a word. Oh, mummy, mummy, how could you!' Ory threw herself into a chair where she squirmed painfully.

'Why should I have sullied your fantasies before it was necessary? Get up, Ory, you are ruining your dress on those cupboards.'

Ory did as she was told, but looked at her mother with a hurt, questioning expression.

'Then why can't I stay at home just this one night?' said Ory desperately, as she paced the floor, biting her handkerchief. 'Why all the arrangements to stay with grandma Riber? Why, mother, when I have pleaded with you to let me stay here.'

'But, my dear Ory, we couldn't very well have left Riber at his hotel on his wedding night. Even just for the sake of gossip, we couldn't have done that.'

'But tell me one thing,' Ory stood quietly before her mother, 'do you suppose we'll have separate sleeping cabins aboard his ship?'

'I should think you would. The *Orion* is, after all, one of the largest ships we have.'

Ory studied her mother's expression with a steadfastness that made the older woman avert her eyes.

'I know what you are doing!' exclaimed Ory, almost threateningly. 'You are conspiring against me – all of you!'

'And this is supposed to be a bride . . .' Mrs Ingstad sighed and looked in bewilderment at her daughter, who was again pacing the floor.

'Why didn't you tell me about this beforehand, mummy, when I still had time to save myself?'

'I really thought that girls nowadays knew quite a bit about these things. Had it been in my youth . . . but his is 1869!'

'I know nothing,' said Ory faintly. 'Hally once told me that to get children one had to be alone with one's husband at night. But that sounded like a lot of nonsense to me.'

'Just you be a good girl, Ory, then everything will work out for the best. It is not as bad as you seem to think.'

'You used the word "sully",' cried Ory. 'You said you didn't want to "sully" my fantasies. Oh, mummy, how could you, my own mother, do this to me?'

'It is for your own good, my dearest daughter. Entirely for your own good. And it is my duty to tell you that it is your husband who from now on has you in his charge. Humour him and be as good as a little lamb, otherwise he'll be badly served by his sweet, little wife. And, what's more, you will be acting against God's wishes.'

Ory clenched her handkerchief hard and said nothing.

'But, come now, we really can't stay here any longer.'

'Oh, God, what shall I do,' muttered Ory.

'Why is Ory crying, mummy?' came a sleepy voice from one of the beds and a small boy sat up.

'Go back to sleep, Einar,' Mrs Ingstad went over to the bed and pushed him back on his pillow.

'But, why is Ory crying?' he repeated crossly.

'Ory only wants to have a look at all of you before she leaves.'

'Has the *Orion* come for her now then?'

'No, the *Orion* is in London, as you know. Riber and

Ory will go there to board her.'

'Come over here then, Ory!' said Einar impatiently.

Ory knelt down by his bed and took his head between her hands.

'When I'm older I can sail on the *Orion* too – can't I, Ory?'

'Only if you promise not to forget me while I'm away. You won't – will you – my dear, sweet Einar?'

'No I won't, but then you must remember all the presents you have promised to bring home with you. For you are coming home again, aren't you?' he grabbed his sister by the chin and looked severely at her.

'Of course, Einar. And you can be sure that I won't forget any of the things I have promised you.'

'Riber has also promised – will you remind him?'

'Yes,' whispered Ory.

'Ory is still crying, mummy,' exclaimed the boy. 'Listen, Ory,' he grabbed her ear, 'if Riber is not good to you, I'll cut him into a thousand pieces with my knife, as soon as you come back.'

'Shame on you, Einar,' said his mother severely.

'But I'm not crying at all, Einar,' said Ory, trying to make her voice seem cheerful, though not quite succeeding. 'I have a cold coming on.'

'Come now, Ory.'

'No, mummy, please, wait a little!' Einar clasped his hands firmly about Ory's neck. 'We must remember when we write to you not to write Miss Ingstad on the envelope, but Miss Riber. Is that right, Ory?'

'Mrs Riber,' corrected the mother.

'But that makes Ory as old as you, mummy.'

'Bye bye, Einar, my dear little brother. Give my love to Lolly, Letty and Knut when they wake up in the morning.'

While their mother tucked in Einar, Ory went and kissed the other sleeping children. Mrs Ingstad then led Ory, with a firm grasp on her shoulders, into the adjoining room. Ready for her lay a fur-trimmed coat with matching hat and muff. Ory was placed firmly on a chair while her mother knelt in front of her to help her on with the fur-lined boots which had to go on over the silk shoes. Then she wrapped her up in a yellow shawl with plenty of long frills, helped her on with the coat and buttoned it up.

'The hat really suits you! Here is the muff, the gloves are inside.'

'And now, my blessed, dear daughter,' Mrs Ingstad's mouth went pale and thin lips trembled. 'Be good and sensi – ' her voice trailed away and she pressed her daughter to her and tried to stifle her sobs.

'It is no worse for you than for anyone else. Believe me, it is the best way.'

She paused a little before she could go on: 'You've been dreadfully spoilt, not only at home, no, least of all by us, but by everyone else. Remember that, Ory, because life will be different from now on.'

'But, in God's name, farewell my dear, dear child,' again the words almost faded away.

Ory remained rigid and passive. Some red spots had appeared on her white cheeks and her blue eyes were cold.

'It is good to see you calm. You are not afraid any more now, are you, Ory?'

'It doesn't seem to make any difference,' said Ory, her voice strangely shrivelled. 'I haven't said goodbye to daddy.'

'It doesn't matter, I'll tell him for you.'

'Tell Riber I'm ready then,' said Ory dully.

· 2 ·

Shortly afterwards, Ory was driving along with her bridegroom, who sat next to her, but seemingly in his own world. He was stooped forward, his elbows resting on his knees, his overcoat unbuttoned and his hat pushed back onto his neck.

Ory had squeezed herself into the corner of the carriage and pressed her legs against the seat. She was alert for any sound or movement Riber might make and her head was in a whirl with words and odd phrases she had heard: 'subjection to your husband, good as a lamb, nuptial bed, God's decree. . . .' there was an ache in her head and neck.

If only he didn't move – or say anything. She would fend him off – beg him nicely to leave her alone . . .

Her chest felt so tight she could hardly breathe.

Although . . . it would really be better if he did say something. This silence made it seem like doomsday. He was usually very talkative – what was he thinking about?

'Ha, ha, ha,' burst out Riber in a guffaw.

Ory started and a surge of fear coursed through her, but as Riber's laughter became more and more hearty she felt relief and asked him why he was laughing.

'It is that old nincompoop of a priest,' Riber's laughter almost drowned his words, 'when I pulled my hand out of yours, to wipe my head, he had such a surprise that I heard his knees crack.'

'It was rather an unconventional interruption,' said

11

Ory, 'as we were kneeling there in front of him and in the middle of the Lords Prayer.'

'But, you see, he sent a shower over me when he sneezed. I think it is far more unconventional to be blessed with a sneeze.'

Ory had to laugh.

'A wonderful old fellow,' Riber was obviously worked up and in a state. 'I almost cracked up when he shouted: "Get that dog out of my church!"'

'Yes, and in that pompous, bad-tempered voice,' injected Ory.

'Yes, damned bad-tempered,' said Riber and laughed again. 'Damned bad-tempered', he repeated with a dwindling voice, not caring to let go of the subject.

After this they remained in silence for a while. Riber seemed occupied by his thoughts and Ory's fear returned. Not even her parents, who were so old and knew each other so well, slept together in the same bed . . .

'Say something, Aurora,' the voice cut the silence like a whipcrack. 'You seem so indifferent. Let me at least hold your hand.'

Ory gave him her hand. He rolled the unbuttoned glove down to her fingertips while covering her hand with kisses and moved closer to her. Ory made herself as small as possible until she was sitting more on the carriage wall than on the seat.

'What is wrong with you?' asked Riber and Ory could sense from his tone that his brows were knitted. 'Answer me, Aurora!'

'I don't like being called Aurora,' was all she could muster.

'Is that all! We'll soon see about that. Give me a kiss and I'll call you Ory at once.' He turned abruptly towards her and enveloped her with his massive body.

Ory screamed, 'Don't . . . oh, God . . . don't!'

'I can see we're in for a great time . . .' muttered Riber as he promptly let go of her and moved onto the opposite seat.

12

'You did the same last night when you said good night,' whimpered Ory, 'but you mustn't.'

'Is that why you've been acting strangely all day and didn't even want to squeeze my hand when the old man was reading out the blessing?'

'Yes, that as well,' nodded Ory.

'Bah!' exclaimed Riber. 'What a lot of nursery gibberish!' He slumped into his seat, muttering to himself, but only a moment later he straightened himself up and said cheerfully: 'What can I do to get you in a good mood, Ory? Shall I jump out of the carriage and leap and bound after you in somersaults?' he made as though to push open the carriage door.

'You must be mad!' burst out Ory and grabbed him by the arm. Just then the carriage turned into a cobbled street and Ory could no longer hear what Riber said.

A few moments later they stopped outside grandma Riber's house.

Riber helped Ory out of the carriage and she rapidly ascended the stone steps. At the same instant the door opened and grandma Riber, who had gone on ahead to be able to receive the newly-weds, was reaching out her hand to her daughter-in-law. She stood stiffly erect, in a tight-fitting purple silk dress with three white ostrich feathers on her head, silhouetted against the light in the hall, which was shining in Ory's eyes.

'Welcome,' she said in her tired voice. 'Dear Adolph,' she turned at once to her son, 'you are the last one of my boys I'm marrying away. I hope you will never regret it.' She embraced him briefly, before letting her hands dwell loosely on Ory's shoulders.

'Ane!' she called out behind her at a door which was open in the background.

A grey-haired, skinny maid in a white, frilly cap and with a long white apron on top of her black Sunday dress, appeared with a lit candle in her hand.

'Congratulations Captain Adolph and congratulations,

Miss,' she said and made two abrupt, little curtsies with her stiff, old legs.

'Thank you, Ane,' Riber gave her his large, well-proportioned hand. 'For as long as I can remember you've been around to look after me. If I should die before you, you can claim a pension when my estate is settled up.'

'Oh, Captain Adolph, sir, thank you, but your good mother has already looked after me with a pension. Not to mention all the gifts you have brought home for me over the years – it's quite enough, sir. Yes, Miss, you will hardly believe what a gentleman you have found for a husband.'

'Miss, by the way, is "Madam" now,' observed grandma Riber sharply. 'Won't you let Ane show you the way to your room, Aurora. She will assist you if you need anything – and I'll be up shortly to say good night. For the time being, Adolph, you and I can have a chat in your room.'

Ane went ahead up the long, steep staircase with the light, and Ory followed behind. She got caught up in her dress and had to grab hold of the banisters not to fall.

'Shall I walk behind you, Miss?' asked Ane with concern.

'No, thank you, Ane, we're almost there now.'

They entered a room at the rear of the house, lit by four large candles placed in sparkling silver candlesticks. Two tall windows, draped in homemade filigree curtains that were closely drawn in front of the blinds, covered almost the entire wall opposite the door. More white drapes swathed the enormous double bed which dominated the room. A dressing-table in the corner, the chairs and the chest of drawers were likewise clad in white and a fire blazed noisily in the massive iron stove with its relief work of cherubs and wild animals.

'Isn't this a beautiful wedding chamber, Miss?' asked Ane, holding her light up to all four corners of the room. 'Madam has arranged it all by herself, although I've been allowed to help her with some little things. It seems to me

14

such a solemn business and when we went about it I couldn't help but feel sad.'

'Yes, it's very pretty,' whispered Ory from between pale lips.

'And believe me, Miss, the bed is a delight.' Ane put down her candle and pulled back one of the drapes that surrounded the bed. 'Just like snow. A bride's supposed to be buried in white – if you'll excuse me saying so, Miss, it is, after all, a little like a burial – leaving one life and starting a new one. There's a white cover even on the quilt, with lovely lace, made by Captain Adolph's own dear, departed grandmother.'

'The quilt,' said Ory, standing in the middle of the floor and suddenly stopping in her tracks. 'Is there only the one?'

'What more do you want? Newly-weds always snuggle down together anyway.'

'Well I never . . .' Ane stopped short and concern manifested itself in her face. 'Are you scared, Miss?'

'Yes, Ane, I can't help it,' Ory started to cry through clenched teeth.

'Poor little thing,' said Ane, embracing Ory and stroking her back soothingly. 'What we don't know we always fear – us frail human beings. Especially a wee birdie like yourself, Miss. But bear in mind that it is the Lord who has said: "the twain shall be one flesh."'

'Please, Ane, don't say things like that,' pleaded Ory with a shudder. 'It sounds horrible.'

'Don't worry, Miss. Throw yourself into it and it will soon be over and done with. The sooner the better. But, Miss, we have to make a move now with getting you undressed; we'll have madam here any moment.' She helped Ory off first with the coat and then with the veil and the other accessories, which she folded carefully and placed on top of the chest of drawers.

'You may go now, Ane, I'll manage the rest by myself.'

'Of course you can't, Miss. The dress is buttoned at the back.'

'All right, but that's enough,' said Ory when she had been helped out of the dress. 'I'd really rather do the rest by myself.'

'As you like, Miss – good night then – ' she reached out her hand.

'Thank you, Ane.' Ory received her hand warmly, 'You've brought solace to me tonight.'

'May God Our Father be with you, lass, and guide you on the thorny path that is life,' Ane's voice trembled. 'Good night and sleep well. We will, of course, be seeing each other in the morning before you and Captain Adolph leave.' She slipped out through the door with her candle.

No sooner had Ane left than Ory kicked off her shoes and jumped into bed, still corseted and wearing her train. She pulled the quilt right up to her chin and lay there tensely listening.

Grandma Riber entered only moments later.

'Very good, Aurora. Then everything is all right. I'll look after the bouquet and the veil for you, but the dress – if you'd like to take it along there is room in the small suitcase.'

'No, thank you,' said Ory unhesitatingly. 'It's better left here with you, grandma Riber.'

'As you wish. I'll take good care of it. Then there is nothing else for the time being . . .' she looked about the room searchingly, but nodded with satisfaction.

'Good night, my dear, new daughter,' she bent over the bed and kissed Ory's cheek. 'I hope, if only for Adolph's sake, that we shall have pleasant times together. And, just another small thing, dear, do not call your husband "Riber" – he doesn't like it.'

'No . . .' mumbled Ory.

The old lady left and as on cue, Riber entered immediately after. He still wore his coat unbuttoned and the cap pushed back onto his neck.

He threw a stolen glance at the bed and started to undress hurriedly and with shaking hands.

Ory watched him as through a white haze behind

almost closed eyes. She pressed her hands against her corset and felt its tightness, at the same time registering a large white form that at regular intervals threw things onto the chairs and the table.

'Shall I blow out the lights?' a subdued voice reached her.

'No, don't,' came the answer, abrupt as a recoil.

'As you wish, my darling,' Riber approached the bed and entered.

In the same instant, Ory jumped out and stood on the floor, where she grabbed her fur coat, put it on and went to sit by the furthest away window.

'Well, I'll be damned, I've never seen anything like it,' exclaimed Riber in amazement. He was sitting up in bed, following her every move in utter disbelief. 'Here am I, as restrained and considerate as is humanly possible. Think of what you might have got yourself into with someone of another disposition!'

Ory didn't answer. Her frightened eyes didn't leave Riber for a second and she had drawn up one of her knees which she was clutching with both hands.

'What a delightful wedding night this is!' said Riber after a while with a slow chuckle, as he let his head fall back against the pillow.

About ten minutes must have lapsed in absolute silence. Ory drew each breath soundlessly and with caution. Riber didn't stir.

'Listen, Ory,' Riber broke the silence and turned onto his side the better to see her. 'Do you intend to spend the whole night sitting there?'

Ory nodded.

'Then I can't think of anything better to do than to tell you a ghost story. Would you like that?'

'Oh, no, please don't,' said Ory and huddled further into her coat.

'Well, I'll tell it to you anyway, it might divert your attention a little, which is what you need. And, it is a peculiar story.'

'It happened one night in the Channel on the first trip after my father's death. We had run into a bit of bad weather on the mid-watch and I had been on deck for a couple of hours. About five o'clock I went below deck to my cabin – the saloon I've told you about with the copper stove in the corner – the hatches were off the stern windows since the weather had been exceptionally fine. Daylight was approaching, a grey light seeped through both the windows and the skylight. Just then I noticed a tall, thin figure wearing a lieutenant-colonel's uniform standing, leaning against the mantelpiece and staring at me with tiny, horrible phosphorescent eyes. I shrank back a little when I first looked at the fellow, but then my eyes fell on his immaculately polished boots and it dawned on me that it was actually my father. In my earliest memories I've always associated him with these shining boots, which he managed to keep polished like a mirror even in the most abysmal of Bergen rain. And, if you can try to imagine it, Ory, once I'd recognized him I was thrown into such confusion that I completely forgot that he was dead and it seemed quite natural for him to be there.

' "Father," I said and approached him. "When did you come on board?" But he didn't answer; he just turned around and pointed with a straight arm at the stern windows. Then he looked at me again and the look was threatening, but at that moment he just faded away, right in front of my eyes and had soon vanished in a luminous circle of yellow fog.'

'You frighten the life out of me,' Ory cried out and rushed to the bed.

'But to think I handled a ghost that nonchalantly,' mused Riber, totally given to the recollection. 'The old man must have considered it rude. I think that is why he threatened me.'

'Oh, I'm scared,' said Ory tensely.

'Come, sit here on the bed and let me hold your hand,' suggested Riber 'you'll feel much better for it.'

'It was, I thought, strange that he should point just to

18

those windows,' continued Riber thoughtfully. He shook his head as though to rid himself of the absent look in his eyes and added: 'There have been times when I've considered jumping out through them as the only possible solution.'

'You are crazy!' exclaimed Ory. 'Why?'

'Oh, because I've had trouble with the crew or the officers, or the wind has been particularly contrary and we haven't stirred day in, day out. I can't stand that.'

'How do you mean?' asked Ory in surprise.

'There was a skipper from Mandal who once upon a time ended his life that way,' recollected Riber still with the same vacant expression on his face. 'But that must have been about a hundred years ago. He was probably delirious the poor bloke.'

'Or he may have been insane,' said Ory.

'It comes to the same thing, but hell, why should I be thinking so much about that silly idiot – what has he got to do with me?'

'No, I can't see what he should have to do with you,' agreed Ory. She was holding firmly onto Riber's hand and stroking it slowly.

'But listen now, my sweet, little Ory, you really ought to come into bed. We have to be up bright and early in the morning and the whole night is going.' He unbuttoned her coat and wanted to help her out of it. 'Come, Aurora, let me have you as I have a right to.'

A mixture of fear and bravery flitted across Ory's face.

'Yes, of course, Riber,' she said convincingly. 'Just wait a moment.' She rose from the edge of the bed where she had been perching and grasped her hat from off the small table by the window.

'What do you want with your hat?'

'There's a draught in the hall,' replied Ory and disappeared through the door with one of the candles in her hand. She ran down the steps to the front door where she put the light beside her on the floor while she looked and listened tentatively all around her. She turned the key carefully in the lock, opened the door and let it slam shut behind her.

Outside in the street she started at first to run, but as she gathered her wits she realized that it would be wiser to walk and not arouse the suspicion of the night-watchman.

She headed straight for home.

Riber, who had heard the front door slam, had immediately leapt out of bed and thrown on some clothes. With his overcoat slung across his arm he rushed through the house and onto the street where he caught up with her in no time at all.

'Aurora,' he gasped, out of breath, and grabbed her by the arm. She stopped, fearful and yet surprised at the mixture of tenderness and authority in his voice.

'Aurora, what have I done for you to carry on like this? Why do you want to shame me? I have respectfully and honestly asked you to be mine, because I love you and I have considered having you as my wife my greatest, indeed my only, goal. And you have taken me for your husband. Have you then no feeling of commitment and responsibility?'

Ory hung her head.

'What do you think your parents would have said if you had returned home now? For I suppose that is where you intended to go?'

Ory's chin virtually sank into her chest.

'But, Aurora, if you really don't want me, then for God's sake go back home. Just give it some thought before you do. It will cause a scandal throughout Norway.'

Ory straightened her head, threw it back and looked up at the starlit heaven with roaming eyes, while she muttered something that sounded like a curse.

'Now then, what's it going to be: Yes or no?' his voice was firm, almost commanding, and he reached out his hand to her.

Ory put her hand in Riber's and followed him.

'Remember that I am going to be your guardian and

provider, as well as your father, mother, sisters and brothers . . .' whispered Riber, bending over her 'and I have a heart to be all that and even more for you, Ory.'

Ory nodded almost imperceptibly. A feeling of her own impending doom crept into her and her fear became unimpassioned and lame. Riber was in the seat of power. Revolt would be futile.

When they once again entered the wedding chamber with the grand old ceremonial bed, she undressed quietly and got in. The next moment found her tightly embraced by Riber's strong arms.

· 3 ·

'Aren't you hungry, Mrs Reiber?'

Ory turned away from the window where she had sat for hours in dull contemplation of the uniform grey but exceedingly noisy swarm of people in Cheapside and answered: 'No, thank you.'

'You still prefer to wait for dinner until your husband returns?'

'Yes,' Ory nodded and the landlady of the boarding-house disappeared.

She was a ghastly apparition with her pieccs of false hair that looked as though they were made of waxed, black linen thread and covered all her forehead and a good part of her shappy cap. During the past hour she had called about every ten minutes, stealthily creeping up in her felt shoes, putting the same question in her coarse Irish accent and consistently mispronouncing her name: 'Aren't you hungry, Mrs Reiber?'

Had it not been better to suffer another day of being, as the saying goes 'shown London' by the broker's son, rather than stay here? Even although he was exasperatingly boring and always answered her questions monosyllabically and with an unbearable Swedish accent: Jo' var's, min fru'.

But what could be worse than spending a whole day shut up in this horrible room, with its sickening smell of coal fumes, dark and dingy and with cumbersome horsehair furniture that had probably never been aired or beaten. If she wanted to move even just a chair, ever so slightly, she had to use both hands.

The row from the street was dreadful. She had never imagined that people could live with such a racket going on. It was far worse than the roar of a street fire at home.

She rose and paced slowly up and down on the thick carpet, contemplating the colourless, worn patches in front of the sofa and under the square table in the middle, now laid for two.

How shoddy it all was, the heavy furniture, the lined curtains of auburn velvet with their ornamental borders in tatters – she had been struck at first by the solid, poised feel of the room, but now . . .

She could no longer enjoy the fireplace with its cool, marble surround and the sparkling brass fender that had enchanted her so much at first, not even with a fire glowing in it, as it was doing now. She only noticed the grease that covered the large embossed mirror above it so thickly that one could barely discern the blurred reflection of the gas chandelier which was mirrored in it. The artificial flowers and gaudy, stuffed birds which ornamented the mantelpiece were virtually eaten away by grime.

'Listen – isn't that the woman again?' Ory said to herself. She hurried back to the window and assumed hastily the posture she had been in before, as though she had committed a crime by walking on the floor. She felt like hiding, crawling under the sofa – if only there had been a key to the door!

The gas lamps had been lit outside, spaced evenly in a row on either side of the street and the trams, omnibuses and all manner of other vehicles that were monotonously and continually passing by added their red, green and yellow lights.

Riber seemed to be unusually late today. The meal was due at four o'clock, now it was almost six. Oh, and what a gloomy darkness had descended on the room.

Resting her head in her hand she let herself drift once

more into the sad reflections that had troubled her all day.

God knows, she had been reckless to go and get married so young, or even to get engaged. It almost amounted to the same thing, because as soon as they were engaged people had told her that she could not expect to keep him waiting much longer.

If the incident on the skating-rink back home had not taken place, she would probably have said 'no' when he proposed. But the way he had been the only one brave enough to run across the ice and save the little boy who had fallen headlong into that treacherous, black hole, had excited her. All the others had just stood and stared.

Besides, she could have been a lot worse off than with Riber. He was kind and decent and so much in love that she would have to be made out of stone not to be moved by it. Only one thing seemed wrong, the way he would work himself into a rage sometimes over virtually nothing. At times like that he would rant and rave like a lunatic.

But it was still ungrateful of her not to be happier – *that* must be what bothered Riber.

'Dear God in heaven,' she whispered, 'please help me to love Riber the way you have commanded. You must know how much I want to – help me then for Jesus' sake, you who are almighty.'

If she prayed like that every day then things eventually had to come right.

'Be one flesh,' . . . one flesh with a big, fat, thirty-year-old man! Oh no . . . she didn't like those words at all.

Three short, sharp taps sounded on the door knocker.

Ory shot up and ran fumbling along in the darkness across the floor, into the hallway and up the stairs with their many and spacious landings. On reaching the bedroom she threw herself into the double bed and curled up behind its heavy drapes.

Despite the carpet on the stairs, Ory could sense silent steps approaching in her wake and then she heard the landlady's voice: '. . . Mrs Reiber must have gone upstairs. Would you like me to light the way with a candle, sir?'

Riber answered in a tense voice: 'No, thank you, ma'am. I'll take the candle myself.' Shortly after that the bedroom door opened and a strip of pale yellow light fell across the patterned carpet.

'Come on out, Ory!' his voice was gruff. 'What's all this nonsense?!'

'But I haven't hidden,' said Ory feebly, as she quickly left her hiding place. 'I only came up here to wash my hands.'

'It seems to me you could have managed that earlier. It's six o'clock, I'm home late, I'm hungry and exhausted and still I have to wait for my dinner. What are you playing at?'

'Me – playing at – ?' Ory looked crestfallen.

Riber, who was pacing the floor, stopped suddenly just in front of her and said in an earshatteringly loud and angry voice: 'Then why wouldn't you go out with young Mr Brandt today? Wasn't that because you'd rather play the martyr? I can see that you've been weeping – don't deny it!'

'But I haven't complained about anything,' said Ory unsteadily.

'Of course not. You are too proud to come to me with your complaints, but I can well imagine what it is you write home about.'

'That is not true, Riber,' said Ory indignantly. 'I have never done anything of the sort.'

'Riber,' he imitated her voice. 'Riber, Riber, Riber . . . why must you call me Riber – when I'm not Riber! My father was Riber – I'm Adolph! Are you listening?'

'Are you assuming that I'm deaf?'

'You are as stubborn as a mule,' he continued in the same loud, piercing voice with each word reverberating. 'Let me see if I can get you to call me Adolph, if only just once for all the times I've asked you. Even old Ane calls me Adolph; doesn't that shame you a little?'

26

'I will when I get used to it,' said Ory slowly.

'What a load of nonsense!' Riber seemed to shrink inside his clothes and shook himself in revulsion. 'Damn marriage! It ought to be punishable.'

Ory looked at him in astonishment.

'The story circulating now, I suppose, will be that I have neglected you in London, left you behind all day in a shoddy boarding-house. It will give your uncle Pitter, the old boozer, something to joke and drivel and rub his nose about, till it's as red as a beetroot. Ha, ha!' he laughed bitterly. 'You won't deny that you've said it was shoddy here, will you?'

'I might well have,' said Ory, 'but I really can't remember.'

'You are an exacting little so-and-so! If you'd seen some of the places I've put up with when circumstances have called for it – but that's women! Oh hell! Why can't one live without them!' He stood absolutely still, but his eyes roamed frantically about the room and came to rest only for a moment on the bed before he threw himself at it and tore a bolster out from underneath the cover. He threw it vehemently on the floor, picked it up and threw it down again and continued until he was out of breath.

Ory had sat down on a stool by the fireplace and watched him with a mixture of fear and anger. When at last he kicked the pillow with a final almighty effort which left him spent, she hid her face in her hands.

There followed a knock on the door and the landlady peered in: 'Dinner is ready, sir.'

'All right,' Riber brushed her away with his hand.

'I have a lot of problems on my hands just now,' began Riber anew and started to walk slowly up and down. 'The officers have been lazy and have been living it up, which has cost the company the earth while I've been away getting married. What a mess! Today while I was in town on business, the first mate refused to load a consignment of cargo. But I'll teach the rogue – I'll show him a thing or two his mother never did. Now, of course, he's trying to make it look as though I'm neglecting the company's interests because I've brought my wife along. But not for an instant will you, my good woman, get in the way of my business!' The top half of his body swayed menacingly towards Ory, his hands embedded in his trouser pockets and he transfixed her with a fierce stare. 'Do you hear me? Why in God's name didn't you stick to your decision to delay marriage till the New Year. I would have brought the ship home by then and everything could have been different.'

Ory raised her head and looked at him.

'Yes, go on – have a good look! The ship is losing a lot of money for the sake of all this tomfoolery – and try as I might, I can't even say I'm having a good time.'

The door opened once again.

'I'm afraid dinner will be spoilt, sir,' said the landlady curtly.

'Thank you!' shouted Riber. 'We're coming down at once, ma'am.'

He walked over to the double washstand, poured water into one of the ample basins, bathed his face thoroughly in it and finally washed his hands. While he dried himself he looked at Ory and asked at last in a feeble and embarrassed voice: 'Are you asleep, Aurora?'

She neither answered, nor stirred.

'Let's go, Ory. It's about time we had something to eat. Otherwise our orang-utang landlady will explode which will make the whole house come tumbling down upon us.'

'Don't sit there sulking, Ory,' continued Riber amiably. 'You don't want the old girl downstairs to notice anything, do you?'

'Or maybe that is what you want – to create another scene?' At this his voice had become impatient.

'I – create a scene?' Ory lifted her head questioningly.

'Well, you or me – it amounts to the same. You must have realized, Ory, what I'm like. Anger gets a hold of me, but once it's out – it's over and done with. Come now.'

28

Ory got up wearily. Riber wanted to hug her, but she pulled away and walked ahead of him down the stairs. The gas chandelier was lit above the table.

During the meal not a word was exchanged between them. Ory was pale and her features drawn; she could hardly get down a bite. Riber was chatting genially with the landlady who served oxtail soup, roast beef and plum pudding, while keeping their glass mugs topped with a mixture of stout and pale ale she had ready-mixed in a jug. At every other mouthful she expressed her concern that 'dinner' should be according to their taste.

When they had finished she cleared the table and put a carafe of port in front of Riber. He poured out two glasses and lit a cigar.

'Well, I'll be leaving you then,' said the landlady 'should you be requiring anything else, Captain Reiber, sir, just ring the bell.'

As soon as she was out of the room, Ory rose and headed for the door.

'Don't you want a glass of port, Ory? Please, be a good girl.'

Ory shook her head and went upstairs, where she again sat down on the small stool by the fireplace. The candle by the washstand was burning restlessly, making the big pieces of furniture cast shapeless, long shadows on the carpet.

She felt numb to the core of her being.

What kind of a human being *was* Riber? His explosions came always with the unexpectedness of a shower from a clear sky. This morning when he had left he had seemed the picture of a contented man – only to return like this.

But then she really did not deserve any better – it was actually nothing but a reflection on her own behaviour. She was far from that which a loving wife ought to be. Whenever he approached her with his love, she was cold and unyielding – 'always indisposed' as he had coined it. And that was the sad truth.

But why did he have to say so many horrible things in

his anger?! It was of little use that he repented afterwards – it left some gall behind all the same.

She had always wanted and looked forward to seeing the big, beautiful world – yet loneliness and confusion were the only experiences she had received so far. Riber was so thoroughly fed up and bored with it all that he could not have cared less about his surroundings. He was only content at sea or when he was home with grandma Riber. Nobody had told her or shown her anything whatsoever. She felt as lost in the crowds here as she had done when as a small child she had been taken along to see the tableaux.

'The easiest thing in the world is to be the wife of a man who is in love,' her mother had once said and probably added in her thoughts: 'Then he can be manipulated into doing one's own bidding.'

Oh, but it was not that simple.

Even had she had the greatest of love in store it would soon have been ground down in the face of this. Yet here she was with absolutely nothing to go on, struggling along hour by hour, praying to God for a will and a way to love her husband as she ought. How on earth would she manage on the forthcoming journey? Alone on the ocean with this strange and unpredictable person.

'. . . alone on the ocean . . .' the thought filled her heart to overflowing and brought on the tears, large and hot.

Tired and despondent she leaned her whole body against the fireplace and dozed off.

She was woken by a light touch. Startled out of sleep, she saw Riber standing in front of her.

'I'm sorry, Ory. I meant nothing of what I said,' he bent over her and laid his arms on her shoulders.

'Let me get up – I'm sitting uncomfortably.'

'Are you uncomfortable?' he straightened up at once.

Ory got up and limped across the floor. Riber wanted to help her, but she fended him off: 'It's only my leg that's asleep,' she sat down on the chest at the foot of the bed.

'Let me hear you say that you forgive me, Ory,' Riber pleaded in a piteous voice.

'It's all the same to me,' said Ory, snubbing him.

'As far as I know there is no more a man can do when he's overstepped, than to ask for forgiveness.'

'The same can be said for a lout,' answered Ory with contempt.

'You know, Ory, how I love you,' whimpered Riber. 'I will do anything for you.'

'Then you may start by being altogether different,' blurted out Ory. 'You have no reason to treat me the way you do.'

'No, I know,' said Riber. He had taken her former seat by the fireplace.

'I'm not exactly having a good time either,' continued Ory in a tremulous voice. 'You know a lot of people and can talk with whom you wish, while I. . . . Even if you battered me to death there would be no use in me screaming for help.'

'What kind of thought is this?' Riber was by her side in a stride. 'Do you think I would ever be capable of hurting you, Ory?'

'Huh!' said Ory and turned away her head.

'I assure you I would rather have myself thrown to the lions than to harm a single hair on your head. Ory, sweet Ory, you know – no, you can't possibly know, how I love you,' he was close to tears and the knuckles were white on his clenched fists. 'You are the only one in the world who could cause me grief and the only one who can give me any real pleasure. If one day you decided to pull off my beard, I would kiss your hands for doing it. Hit me in the face, Ory. I beg you – hit me in the face.'

Ory almost had to laugh, but managed to constrain it with an effort.

'Every word I say is true, Ory, you must believe me.' Riber still loomed above her, staring steadily down at her with his small, slant eyes which expressed a fervent devotion. 'You don't know it, but I have more than once thought of killing myself for your sake. I don't think I'm good enough for you. I don't make you happy, which you deserve to be and I'm afraid I won't improve with age. There is something bad and irrepressible in my nature – although there certainly is good in me as well. I swear by God the Almighty, that I've thought of killing myself for your sake.'

'Please, be quiet now,' exclaimed Ory with an involuntary shudder. 'You always go to extremes whether for good or bad when you have one of your fits.'

'How else should it be?' continued Riber in the same meek and beseeching manner and without having heard a word of what Ory had said. 'You are as innocent as one of God's angels and I am a dirty sinner. I never knew that a young girl could be as you are, Ory. Your goodness would make my death a worthwhile sacrifice.'

'Oh, no, Riber, don't say things like that – I am not like that, I am not as good as you think.' She reached out her hands to him as her face dissolved in tears.

'Oh yes, Ory, my love, my Divine Revelation, you are all the things I say you are. You don't know what good you've done me. Through you I've become a better human being – or I'm on the right path at least. Don't you believe me?'

'I don't know, Riber. You frighten me so often.'

'Because I'm a monster, Ory. My grandfather on my father's side was also like that – I've got it from him and, of course, fifteen years at sea hasn't improved matters. A seaman's life doesn't bring out the best in a boy of that age. This afternoon I've been getting all worked up about the first mate, but there is something about that fellow which prevents me laying into him. I don't know what the devil it is.'

'And then I had to get it instead of him,' said Ory with a sigh and dried her eyes with a handkerchief.

'Partly that. But it was more that I was angry with myself. I'd been sitting for more than two hours in a pub, knowing that you were waiting for me, talking nonsense with a captain from Arendal and some woman he was with.'

'A woman – what kind of a woman?'

'Oh, a proper English tart. He whisked her off at last, otherwise I might have been there still. God bless his appetite, I must say. He's got his wife with him as well, the letcher, she's a dainty, fun-loving little thing of about twenty-two.'

'And you talk to women like that?' Ory shot up from her seat with a sudden hardening of her features that took Riber quite aback.

'How could I have avoided it, my Ory? Especially here in London where they approach one all the time and do their best to hang on. Well, Ory, what can I say – it would be virtually impossible not to talk to any of them – '

'Oh, Riber – you haven't ever . . .' she threw her arms about his neck and he could feel her heartbeat racing along.

'My sweet Ory – I will tell you everything from my past – everything you care to listen to that is. I have, thank God, nothing to hide or to be ashamed of.'

Ory straightened up: 'Tell me then – begin at once.'

'No, not tonight – there's plenty of time. Now we're going to go out and have fun. We need a little gaiety after a day like this.'

'Let's not – I'd rather we stayed at home,' said Ory, breathing on her handkerchief and dabbing her eyes soothingly with it.

'Not likely, my treasure. We'll go to the Alhambra or to the theatre or anywhere else you wish. And listen, Ory! Wear the red velvet dress I bought you the other day and the lace collar. I want to show off my beautiful wife.'

Riber lit the candles on the dressing-table and fetched her tall, button-up bronze leather boots, opened the suitcase, pulled out the drawers and filled the basin with water.

'There, my pet, I've prepared everything for you. When

33

we're on board I'll first and foremost be at your disposal as chambermaid, secondly I'll be captain. Here's your dressing-gown – take of your dress – and let me brush and comb your lovely hair.'

'That would take too much time,' objected Ory, besides, her hair was in perfect shape.

'He's a dear person all the same,' considered Ory as she changed. 'Not particularly handsome, although in his bearing he can be said to be elegant at times.' She watched him as she buttoned up her dress, brushing his beard and twirling his moustache, talking to himself in the mirror above the basins. His back was thickset and a slight stoop was accentuated by a pair of braces crossing it. 'But still – tonight she could definitely feel that she was fond of him. Thank God.'

'How pretty you are, Ory,' Riber tilted his head and looked well pleased. 'And how wickedly seductive you look – with those incomprehensible eyes and your pert, young breasts. But why – you witch, can't you be like other women?' He threatened her playfully.

'What do you know about other women?'

'Silly billy,' said Riber laughing and pinched her cheek. But as he became aware of the colour rising in her face, he changed to a serious tone: 'Don't be silly, lass! Where the devil would I know that from?'

· 4 ·

Ory lay awake inside the canopied bed. Her armpits and
chest ached from having her hands stuck beneath her neck
too long. Even so, she didn't bother to change position,
being too engrossed in re-living events of the evening
which went through her mind over and over again.
Throughout her reveries, which tormented her, rhythms
from a never ending Strauss waltz went through her head
and would sweep her along on a soft wave or whirl her
into a frenzy.

Next to her Riber was snoring like thunder.

Ory stared with wide open eyes into the dark. One
moment she was in a brightly lit street and gaudily
dressed women swept past her, their silk garments
rustling and giving off clouds of powder and patchouli.
They greeted each other gushingly, smiling and nodding
with sparkling eyes, lifting their feet up high for every step
they took, their skirts swishing about their legs, their
earrings and other gewgaws tinkling against their soft
tight-fitting velvet coats. They wriggled and squirmed and
outrivalled each other, as though they were the only
actors on the stage and one had to manoeuvre with
considerable care not to be bumped into.

Riber had seemed used to them and at ease. With a
squeeze of her arm and a strangely affected voice he had
told her in the midst of it all, that it was an enchanting
feeling to be mingling with this gaudy trash with her
there, securely at his side, a sweet, innocent woman, who

forever more was going to be his amulet against all this depravity.

'Was it different before?'

Had she simply known that Riber had kept away from all that she would not have given it another thought. It was after all none of her business how the rest of the world lived.

But about *him* to whom she was married, she had to know everything. She had, after all, bound herself to love this man for the rest of her life.

'Oh, no, no, no,' she sat abruptly upright and bit the sheet as the tears came flooding over her face: 'Please, Riber, don't tell me you've been like that! Tell me rather that you've been a clean-living, good and honourable young man who saved yourself for the one you were destined to marry.'

Suddenly there came a sharp rattle into Riber's otherwise monotonous snoring. Ory started: Was he giving up the ghost? She lit a match and held it above his face which was heavy with sleep and covered in beads of perspiration. The tip of his fat tongue was protruding from between his teeth.

'You are carrying on terribly, Riber. Is anything the matter?' Ory shook him by the shoulder.

Riber's eyes twitched and one of his lids opened slightly. At the same moment Ory had to put out the match not to burn her fingers. She heard Riber with a dull grunt turn on his side, where he continued to snore.

Ory dried her eyes on the sheet and lay down as she had done before.

She wondered if all men slept the way Riber did, seemingly with their whole bodies. He seemed not to exist as a human being any more, but rather as a lump of lead.

The waltz continued noisily in her weary head, she felt as if she was being pulled along in a rhythmical, lulling motion . . .

It might possibly have been only a casual acquaintance he had had with the slant-eyed woman, the one with the clammy skin and all the pearls, who at the Alhambra had slapped him on the back and said: 'Good evening, Captain Adolph! How are you, dearie?'

But why had he then ducked away and looked embarrassed? He was not usually one for accepting an insult lying down. How terribly unsure of himself he had seemed when in answer to her questioning look he had said: 'Don't let it worry you, Ory, that kind of tart is capable of anything. You won't believe how rude they can be sometimes.'

How could he want to take her along to places like that? It stank of corruption, with people swilling beer and smoking inside the actual theatre and women shouting and banging the tables until they were thrown out by the police. But it might equally well be a sign of a clear conscience.

Good gracious, how he could snore! Sleeping through it would have been impossible even if she had not had all these disturbing thoughts. It was like a mountain splitting. And then occasionally a loud bang, like a champagne cork popping, would emit from his mouth. Or a long drawn-out wheeze like the one that had come from the acrobat at the Alhambra when he had slipped from his trapeze way up under the ceiling and landed with a dull thud on the floor. Oh, the horror of it! Screams from men and women who fainted while the magnificent body in the leotard lay supine and motionless, nose pointing upwards and arms sprawling.

Riber had grabbed her and pulled her out of the theatre saying they were going to go somewhere else. She had sobbed hysterically, been out of her mind and pleaded to go home, but Riber had insisted on finishing the evening on a gay note and had called for a cab in a loud voice.

Excited and feverish, barely able to control herself, she had with burning eyes and pain in her heart watched the seething mass of people and blinding bright lights from the gallery of the dance hall where the cab had deposited them. Large, beautiful, magnificently arrayed women, were frollicking about, their backs naked and their breasts exposed with not a trace of a sleeve on their so-called dresses. They held their sinuous bodies close against well-dressed gentlemen of all ages, neighing and whinnying, sounding like cats screeching through the heady Strauss waltz. Whenever one of the men wanted to engage a woman for a dance, he'd stroll up to her, pince-nez perched upon his nose, better to see the lady's bare limbs before making his final choice, when he caught the woman's attention by putting his walking stick onto the tail of her dress.

This was how they had finished the evening 'on a gay note'. This is what Riber called gay!

She felt an icy shudder run up her spine when she thought of how he, with flared nostrils, had been drinking in the queer, sickly smell of human being, mixed with a scent of perfume and flower, a wan smile hovering about his lips and making his vaguely trembling moustache move up and down as he whispered: 'Look Ory – look! Fabulous! Brilliant! This is yet another side of life that has to be learnt.'

Good heavens, no! He'd never get her to put her foot inside places like that again. It was as though she had seen the root of all evil, visited Satan's own domain. She felt overcome by it, as though she had contributed to the sin and vice merely by being an onlooker.

She threw herself about in the bed and closed her eyes firmly trying to induce sleep, but the oppressive visions haunted her and she could not get the rhythm of the waltz out of her head. He had looked at her pityingly and shrugged his shoulders when she had asked where the couples went when they disappeared through the entrance, sometimes in a tight embrace with the woman half carried by the man.

'You are too naive, Ory. I don't know what to tell you,' and he had twirled his moustache in a supercilious way that had made her want to slap him.

'You are too naive, Ory.' The answer implied a

knowledge of the depths of sin and shame.

Yes, it certainly had been a gay evening!

And it had continued like that to the very end.

At the oyster house in Maiden Lane where there were stalls on both sides of the wide aisle, with velvet covered seats and marble tables, still another event was to take place, that had pierced her heart. On their way through the premises, where all the seats seemed to be occupied, Riber had been accosted by a woman in green velvet who was sitting all alone in one of the stalls with a large glass of port in front of her. Riber had walked past her without answering and a waiter had brought chairs and a table to a spot where he had managed to fit them in, next to the bar. A woman with golden yellow hair and a blue satin dress presided over the bar, a pyramid of bottles loomed behind her and on the sumptuous buffet in front of her, were all manner of silver dishes and cut crystal.

Twice, the woman in green velvet had stepped out of her stall and examined them rudely, making Ory wish she could sink into the ground. She had wanted to take it up with Riber, but he had acted as though nothing was going on, and she could not get the words out for the lump in her throat.

And then Riber had been angry, because, when they eventually got back home, she 'had not been in the mood' as he had phrased it.

After an evening like that!

'One, two, three, four, five,' Ory counted the strokes of the old grandfather clock in the hall.

Only five! She had expected it to have been at least seven o'clock, it felt as though she had been lying here in the dark much longer.

Riber's snoring had become a lot quieter. Periodically she could hear only deep, regular breathing, interrupted now and then by the old thunder, but it had subsided considerably.

As he obviously was capable of it, why didn't he always sleep like that? It was most inconsiderate of him to sleep the way he did when he knew someone else was lying next to him. She would have to tell him about this in the morning. . . .

Shortly after that, Ory dozed off. When she woke up, after a couple of hours heavy sleep, it was with a sensation of being looked at. She rubbed her eyes and focused immediately on Riber, who was looking at her with an exhalted and tender expression.

He had pulled himself halfway out of the covers and rested his elbow on the pillow, supporting his chin in his hand.

'Good morning, my pet,' he said and nodded. 'You are so beautiful when you are asleep that I can't stop looking at you.'

At the same instant Ory threw herself into his arms and started to weep fitfully, her head bouncing on his shoulder with each suppressed sob.

He covered her with caresses while gently and with due surprise enquired of her what was the matter. Ory's only response was to cling harder to him and a long time passed before she got over her crying enough to be able to talk. She had had a terrible dream – she would never forget it – oh, she hoped it would never come true!'

Tucking her into his arm he lay down on the pillow with her to hear the rest.

'No, I can't repeat it,' said Ory and drew closer to him. 'What happened, yes – how it happened, yes – but not – oh, never the fear and horror of it. But I'll try, it sounds like nothing, but still – I'm cold from fear – wait . . . yes. . . .

'It was a summer day. I was walking by myself in the sunshine, wearing a light summer dress. There were pale green birches on either side. . . . Suddenly a gate appeared just a few steps ahead of me. You were on the other side, leaning on it, watching me approach you. Your whole countenance expressed profound sorrow and suffering – Oh, it was heartrending the way your eyes pleaded with me,' she stopped, once again overwhelmed by tears and then she continued: 'I was hard and angry and I just looked at you, although in my heart of hearts I was touched and pitied you.'

'"Ory?" you whispered to me and reached out your hand. You barely managed to force the words out – still I heard them distinctly – "Won't you save me?"

'But I just stood there, looking at you – implacable, merciless. You repeated your question and after a long while you repeated it again and each time your voice grew fainter. Then you started to disintegrate and, growing thin, your face had become ashen. I still said nothing – I felt stubbornly that I didn't want to. You sighed – oh, dear God, it was a dreadful sigh you let out – then you turned round and walked down a narrow path, much narrower than the one on my side of the gate. You were stooped forward, with your hands folded behind your back, walking slowly, stumbling occasionally, towards some derelict houses behind which rose a seemingly endless wall of thick, damp fog. You never stopped or hesitated or turned round and then, like lightning, you were whisked away into the fog.

'At that moment I felt as though a knife pierced my heart. I wanted to run after you – call you back – have you return to me – but I managed neither to move my legs, nor to make a sound. Then, out of the fog appeared a large, arid eye – it came closer and closer and looked at me threateningly, damning me and then I woke up – and, thank heavens, you were here, alive and well, and I had not caused your ruin and death! Oh, Good Lord, how wonderful it is that I really haven't,' and she let out a sigh of great relief as she laid her face on his chest.

'Do you know, Ory,' said Riber, when after a while they sat back to back on either side of the bed, putting on their stockings – 'here in London one needs to bath at least twice a day. The coaldust gets in everywhere.'

· 5 ·

A week had run its course and during this time Riber had
often taken time off to show Ory something of London.
Afterwards they had always ended up going to some
theatre or other. On each occasion Riber had come home
dissatisfied. Ory had been tense and quiet, something
which had acted as a damper on his mood. It might
happen that she seemed happy for a while and took an
interest in something he had shown her, but the next
minute she would change, without him knowing why and
shut up as tight as a clam for the rest of the day. There
was the time when they were caught in a shower in Hyde
Park and Ory had got so drenched that they had gone to a
hotel and taken a room just to dry her clothes. She had
been sitting in front of the fire, apparently quite
contented, laughing at the way he had teased her as he
was pulling off her shoes and hanging them to dry on the
fender. And the whole time, while they had lunch and
talked, she had been bright and lively, until suddenly as
they were walking downstairs on their way out and he
had let slip the seemingly innocuous remark that the first
thing the porter would do when they left, was to see if the
bed had been used. . . . The heavy cloud had descended
on her there and then and he had not had a word nor a
smile out of her again that day. A strange creature indeed,
this Ory. God only could tell what it was she brooded
about.

Sunday arrived. Ory and Riber were invited to dinner

by Høst, the ship's broker, who lived in a red brick villa in one of the London suburbs.

Ory was seated at table with Høst on one side and a Mr Bøhn, a plump, young Norwegian, on the other. He had wealthy parents and worked as an apprentice in the ship-brokers' firm where Høst was one of the principals.

The rest of the party consisted of Captain Smith from Arendal, the one Riber had previously been out drinking with and his petite wife. Another woman in her mid-thirties, fair and extremely pale, was sitting next to Captain Smith. She was apparently a relative of Høst's who had come over from Norway to act as companion for the childless Mrs Høst. Riber's dinner partner was Mrs Høst, who was English by birth.

The dining-room was luxuriously furnished with a Brussels carpet, Gobelin curtains and solid mahogany furniture. There were pictures on the walls and the silver sparkling on the sideboard was reflected in the mirror above. The table itself was resplendent with fruit, flowers, cut-crystal carafes and six glasses at each place.

'As I was saying, madam,' Høst addressed Ory in his languid manner, 'it is all a matter of willpower . . .' he waited, while one of the maids removed his soup plate, '. . . seasickness can be kept at bay.'

'But I don't suffer from seasickness,' said Ory, looking at him with surprise, 'I've just told you.'

'Yes, of course – so you did! Pardon my distraction. All the same, it's a terrible illness. A woman of my acquaintance, who was going to Japan with her husband – '

'Cheers, Mrs Riber!' Captain Smith lifted his glass and winked cheekily at Ory. 'To a successful closer acquaintance.'

'May I join in!' exclaimed his wife. She was wearing a dress of black silk taffeta with a brilliant red velvet rosette at the cleavage. 'Since we are going to the same place I hope we can meet and be friends.'

Ory smiled with her eyes from one to the other, while

she sipped her glass and thought: 'No thank you, my friend! A fellow who runs around with tarts – I wonder what the Høsts would have done if they had known!'

'We are drinking to our mutual friendship with your wife,' called out Captain Smith amiably to Riber, who was talking in English with Mrs Høst.

'Can you imagine it,' Høst's monotonous voice rose, 'she'd been throwing up for six weeks – yes, I'm telling you, six weeks continuously when . . .'

Ory lowered her eyes and assumed an expression of attentiveness, while she thought about the pale, blonde woman across the table. Miss Sanna, as they called her. She had a dimple on one of her cheeks and a scrofulous scar on the other, but what struck one most were her eyes. Ory had never seen eyes of such a clear, brilliant blue colour, nor eyebrows as finely formed. The lids seemed strangely arched and hid almost all the whites, giving the eyes a veiled look and a sad expression, except when they met her own and then they seemed peculiarly threatening.

'Your husband would like with you to drink!' said Mrs Høst in a still awkward Norwegian, her ruddy face leaning forward in an attempt to catch Ory's attention.

Ory blushed as she lifted her glass and drank, throwing a glance at Riber, who smiled at her with his glass held high. She felt that everybody was looking at her and became embarrassed and irritated at Riber, who would not leave her alone.

'He very much is in love with you,' said Mrs Høst, still addressing Ory. 'He don't talk about anything else and I do understand him very well,' she bared two rows of large, white teeth in an admiring smile.

Ory felt the blood rushing to her head and she seized the glass of water, which she almost emptied. As she put down her glass, she looked across the table at Miss Sanna and was met once again by her hostile gaze and her full lips upturned in a repellent sneer. As before, it made her feel uncomfortable and she attempted to return the stare, but was soon forced to give up and had to avert her eyes.

The fish course was finished and the plates were being changed.

'At last there was only blood coming up, blood and gall,' continued Høst.

'Were you seasick coming over here then, madam?' asked Bøhn suddenly in his high-pitched, shrill accent from the east of Norway. Until then he had not uttered a single word, only tucked into the food quietly and drunk great quantities of Rhine hock and Madeira to which he had helped himself. It seemed as though he had suddenly woken up.

Ory started at his unexpected question. A desire to rid herself of the boredom she was feeling and be indulgent, overcame her. With a smile that was at once arch and sulky she answered: 'Do you think it amusing to be asked one and the same thing many times a day by many people?'

'I don't think I understand you – would you care to tell me what exactly you mean?' Bøhn looked thoughtful.

'Just answer – would you find it amusing or not?'

'Would I find it amusing. . . . No, I shouldn't think I would.'

'Nor do I,' said Ory and shook her head with a laugh.

'She was buried in the Pacific,' said Høst to end his story.

'In the Pacific,' exclaimed Ory enthusiastically. 'Buried, – was that what you said?'

'Yes, what else could the husband do? One can't go carrying corpses about. Sanna, dear, hand me the mustard, please. It is, you see, possible to die from seasickness.'

'Who died of seasickness? Someone you knew well?'

'I have just told you,' there was a hint of irritation in Høst's voice. 'A lady of my acqaintance . . .'

'Who was going to Japan with her husband,' continued Ory quickly. 'I was a little confused for a moment. It must have been terrible for her husband and for her as well. Do you suffer from seasickness, Mr Bøhn?'

Bøhn, who had started eating again, had lapsed into silence once more and when he turned towards her looked as though he had been asked a riddle. Suddenly his face brightened and he burst out in a shrill laughter.

'What are you laughing at?' asked Ory in surprise.

'No, no, it is just too funny for words,' panted Bøhn.

'Tell me,' said Ory and leaned towards him.

At those words, Bøhn laughed even more. He got out his handkerchief and wiped his face, while he groaned: 'Mercy on us!'

Now Ory had to laugh as well.

'Ladies and gentlemen,' Høst was standing. His arms were splayed, his knuckles resting on the table, while his somewhat torpid gaze moved slowly from one to the other.

'I hope it is not going to be about us . . .' thought Ory, twisting her hands in her lap. Any reference made to her being newly-wed, or Riber being her husband, seemed to her extremely disagreeable.

'My wife and I . . .' began Høst when he had obtained silence, 'have this evening the rare opportunity of having a newly-wed couple to dine with us.'

'Hear, hear!' attempted Captain Smith, whose small, brown eyes glistened with wine and well-being.

'Marriage is decreed by God,' continued Høst in a low, nasal manner, 'that men and women may be a pleasure and support for each other.' She could see it all coming, all about that institution's advantages . . .

Ory glanced in the direction of Miss Sanna. Fortunately, this time she was looking straight ahead. What's more, it gave Ory a perfect opportunity to study her. Pity about the scar; it was the only fault on her face. Although, her lips . . . they were too thick and arrogant, her teeth, as well, had too many dark fillings, but they obviously did not show when she kept her mouth shut, as now.

'We, my wi – my family and I,' with this correction

Høst's eyes fell upon Miss Sanna's ash-blonde braids –
'have known Captain Riber for a long time and I dare
say, although – yes, even in spite of – well, as I was
saying – even due to divergence or unforeseen circumstances . . .'

Mrs Høst's tight-fitting silk dress rustled. Riber fidgeted
in his chair. Ory looked from one to the other. A red spot
had appeared on Riber's temple, the one which was
turned towards her, and he was tapping his fingers
noiselessly on the tablecloth. Mrs Høst remained with a
fixed smile while her eyes studied the plate in front of her
and Miss Sanna seemed altogether transformed. Her pale
cheeks were as grey as chalk, the scar was larger and
more livid, her face was dead – the only life that remained
was a vague quivering of the nostrils.

'Captain Riber has no better friends than my family
and myself, who heartily congratulate him on the young
and lovable wife he has got. A toast, then, ladies and
gentlemen – to the newly-weds!' Høst lifted his glass of
champagne, clinked it with Ory's and bowed towards
Riber. Smith leapt out of his chair and bowed in all
directions, while Riber rose unwillingly and the others
followed his example, except Mrs Høst.

When the others had sat down again, Riber remained
standing. He let the maid fill his glass, whereupon he
thanked his host in a few words for his speech and helped
himself to a piece of game before he too sat down.

Ory felt relieved. The inexplicable discomfort which
had overcome the party, like a cold draught, during
Høst's speech had now passed off and the talking was as
lively as it had been before.

'What is it Riber is telling you?' Høst asked his wife,
who was shaking with laughter.

'It is a story from the time I was sailing with "the War
Lord",' said Riber casually.

'Where he make a fool his kapitan and sent a
policeman . . .' said Mrs Høst. 'But, please, Kapitan
Riber, you tell yourself.'

'I was given a part in a comedy at Christensen's the ship's chandler in Odessa,' began Riber.

'Ah, the Swede with all the beautiful daughters . . .' interrupted Smith, '. . . and you were a cat among the pigeons, eh!'

'They weren't that pretty, damn it!' protested Riber. 'Anaemic creatures with bad teeth.'

'Ha, ha,' laughed Miss Sanna derisively.

'Not beautiful indeed!' shouted Mrs Smith, wagging her finger at Riber. 'I've heard you were infatuated by all of them. No need to be jealous, Mrs Riber, the Christensen daughters could never have been as beautiful as you are.'

'And then his kapitan would not let him go,' urged Mrs Høst.

'No,' said Riber. 'He swore that he would not let me off the ship that day, not alive at any rate. I told him we'd see about that. I had been to all the rehearsals, you see. They were always held in the evening after working hours and I couldn't very well leave them high and dry on the actual day of the performance. It was to be held at seven, with a ball afterwards. I had two costumes for the play, one for my part and another for a dancing part I was also taking. The day before the play I sent the costumes up to Christensen, while I went ashore myself in the evening and found a policeman I bribed to come and arrest me the next day at five o'clock in the afternoon. The good man arrived promptly and told the captain some tall story and huffed and puffed and pointed at me while he did it. He even read out my name in full from a note and made gestures that showed I had to come with him at once. The two of them must have gone on arguing with signs and finger language for more than half an hour, but at last the captain said I had to leave, there was nothing else for it. On my way down the gangway he assured me that he'd go to the Consulate and make sure I'd be paid damages if I had been wrongly arrested.'

'And then he played komedie and his kapitan was looking on,' interrupted Mrs Høst excitedly.

'Yes, he was invited as audience. My part wasn't until the third act, but when I appeared, you should have heard the captain. "Stop him!" he shouted and stood up, pointing at me. The other people waved at him to sit down again and be quiet and the "War Lord" had to calm down and do as he was asked, while I began my song.'

Everybody laughed. Riber, pleased with himself, looked happily at Ory, while he twirled his moustache.

'Still, the funniest was what followed,' continued Riber. 'We danced into the early hours and when the party was breaking up, the "War Lord" approached me and said: "It's time to go aboard, mate." We went together, but he didn't say a word until we'd reached the gangway, then: "I'll get my own back on you, believe me, Mr Mate!"'

'How did you dare?' shouted Mrs Smith. 'Any other captain, yes – but the "War Lord" who is notorious for his heavy hand. . . .'

'When one's father owns the ship, one might risk a lot that somebody else wouldn't,' said Smith and winked knowingly at Riber.

'My father was not a ship-owner,' answered Riber.

'No, . . . a lieutenant-colonel, of course, I beg your pardon!' Smith laughed. 'Then it must have been your mother or your mother's brother, maybe, it comes to the same thing . . .'

'You've got yourself an endearing husband,' Høst nodded at Ory with his sleepy smile. 'He's one of these people one can never really get angry with.'

'I propose a toast to Mrs Riber, that she may never rub her husband up the wrong way,' said Miss Sanna suddenly and in a derogatory manner, as she clinked her glass angrily against Ory's.

'She really dislikes me, that Miss Sanna,' thought Ory and felt ill at ease.

'My God, madam, you do remind me awfully of Miss Thomsen from Arendal,' exclaimed Bøhn and looked dotingly at Ory. 'Do you know her?'

'Ah, you don't! What I mean to say is that you,

50

madam, are far more beautiful – Miss Thomsen is, in fact, not beautiful at all! But still . . .'

'What is it about her then?' asked Ory, a little put off by Bøhn's intense stare.

'About her? . . Oh, nothing.'

'I thought you were going to tell me something about her.'

'Well . . . I may as well, if you'd like me to. . . . She's been engaged six times.'

'With six different men?'

'Cross my heart, yes! She leads them on on the skating rink.'

'How does she do it?'

'She has her artful little ways . . .' said Bøhn shaking his head disapprovingly.

Ory laughed heartily. 'What an amusing fellow,' she thought before she asked him: 'Are you one of the six?'

'What . . . me? God forbid! I have never been able to stand her, as I've let everybody know. I think she is disgusting to carry on like that.'

'Still, you tell me I remind you of her. Thanks awfully.'

'I assure you – it is a very slight ressemblance. . . . What I meant was that there is something about the nose and the hairstyle, although . . . it may be mainly the figure, but it's quite immaterial. Please don't get me wrong . . .'

'Of course, not,' said Ory cheerfully. 'You needn't apologize. I can see that you only think well of me.'

'Of you, madam . . . yes, good Lord, yes! I'm just sitting here thinking, what a pity it is I'm not a sailor.'

'Why is that a pity?'

'Because if I were I could have asked your husband for a job and gone along with you.'

'Yes, that might have been good fun,' replied Ory, but then she added: 'Although how does one have fun aboard ship?'

'Just to see you every day would be the most delightful thing I could ever imagine.'

'Port or sherry?' asked a maid behind Ory's chair.

'Do have some port, madam,' suggested Høst. 'It is decidedly the best accompaniment to fruit and it's also the healthiest.'

Captain Smith tapped his glass and shot up in the air, like a jack-in-the-box.

'There is a saying that goes like this: "A good deed cannot be done often enough",' he began with a quick, self-satisfied voice, 'That is why I would like before we leave this table to thank our gracious host and his equally gracious lady wife, who have provided us so well, exceedingly well, with good things and also to propose a further toast to the newly-weds, as our host just had the pleasure of doing.'

'The ass,' whispered Ory to Bøhn. 'Go and stuff a serviette in his mouth.'

Bøhn started to giggle. Ory raised her eyebrows and studied her plate, while Smith communicated to the party that it would not be Riber the bridegroom he would address in his speech, but Riber the man and seaman.

Ory suddenly felt something sharp against her ankle, she pulled away her foot, but a moment later it was there again and this time she crossed her legs and pulled them underneath her chair.

'Virtue and clean morals are indeed a blessing,' elucidated Captain Smith, 'and it is my opinion and my experience that marriage is the best guarantee, probably the source from which our virtues and morals spring and the soil they thrive in.'

'The audacity of the man!' thought Ory and when Smith had finished and they were toasting, she raised the glass to her lips without drinking from it.

But what was this? The pushing and prodding had started once more behind her ankles. It must be Bøhn, it came from that direction. Maybe he had dropped something on the floor and was trying to get hold of it with his foot.

'I might as well tell you that it's me you are kicking, Mr Bøhn,' said Ory suddenly and looked at him with a smile.

A deep blush flushed Bøhn's already glowing face. 'Excuse me,' he stammered and knocked over his wineglass. 'I didn't know . . . I thought . . .'

'Can't you keep your long legs to yourself,' murmured Høst in a muffled voice to Bøhn, as he darted a threatening glance towards him out of his half-open eyes.

'It's nothing to get upset about,' said Ory jovially. 'It didn't hurt or anything.' She looked round the table and was happy for Bøhn's sake that nobody else had noticed the incident.

When they had finished eating, everything was cleared from the table and freshly filled carafes of wine, cigars and ashtrays were put there for the men. The ladies, according to English custom, withdrew while the men smoked.

'Shall we for a trip go in the garden?' asked Mrs Høst, when they had finished coffee, looked at all the albums and exhausted their resources of conversation in the drawing-room.

Ory and Mrs Smith wanted to but Miss Sanna excused herself.

A maid brought shawls and headscarves and they went into the garden by way of a conservatory adjoining the drawing-room. It was well stocked with green plants and flowers and the doors leading out into the rather dreary garden had stained glass in them. The early night was moonlit. They walked about on the white, pebbled paths, lined with seashells and rare stones, until Mrs Høst remarked that it was 'cooly' and suggested that they should go back inside.

'Let's walk round the house to the hall,' she said and led the way. 'Then we can leave our shawls there.'

As they walked past the conservatory, where lights had been lit and the walls were almost entirely made of glass, Mrs Smith suddenly exclaimed: 'Well, I do declare. Look Mrs Riber, it seems as though Miss Sanna is giving your husband a piece of her mind.'

Ory turned her head and saw Riber standing inside the

conservatory looking washed out and upset and staring at Miss Sanna, who was sitting in a low armchair, leaning towards him and talking in an agitated manner.

When Ory and the others returned to the drawing-room he was still there, at the same spot in the conservatory, but when they entered he turned round hurriedly and came in and sat down at the table beneath the gas chandelier.

Mrs Høst played and sang for a while. Tea and cakes were served and shortly afterwards the guests started to leave.

The railway station was packed, the compartments were all fairly full and the Smiths and the Ribers were separated.

Ory felt sad and depressed, travelling among foreigners who were either dozing or chatting among themselves in English. An unbearable homesickness overcame her and she turned her head away, not wanting Riber, whose searching eyes she felt to be resting on her, to see that she was fighting back her tears, which kept welling up.

· 6 ·

When they arrived home Ory thought it was too early to go to bed and preferred to sit for a while in their living-room downstairs. Riber lit the gas, put down his hat and coat on the table, before he helped Ory off with hers. Then he sat down in a chair by the door and fell into thought.

He was reflecting on Ory and on his marriage. He couldn't see clearly what was wrong, or why he had so often felt depressed since his marriage. It stemmed, obviously, from Aurora, although she did nothing that annoyed or offended him. It therefore resulted not from her, but from the effect she had upon him, which he assumed was not calculated on her part and something she could do nothing about. That she always seemed depressed or worried was not the real cause either, although that alone was quite enough to make a man feel low, but there was this other thing – he didn't know what to call it – like a wall of pain between them, a strange, somehow threatening pain, a destructive force which filled him with foreboding.

Let me go through this once again, he said to himself, as he supported his cheek in the one hand and his elbow in the other. My heart is full of love towards her. I could even die for her as easily as I eat a sandwich, at least at those times when I'm ecstatic. She, obviously, does not feel the way I do. It would be strange if she did. With my age and my looks I can't expect to arouse such ardent passion from a woman like her. But she is fond of me, which is shown clearly in many little things she does. She is not of a sensual disposition; at least it has not awoken in her yet. It is, however, a disappointment I can bear since it is not caused by a dislike of me, nor of liking someone else better and I am sure that one of these days it will awaken in her. The conclusion must be that there are no obstacles. He drew a deep breath and made himself more comfortable in his chair.

What is it then? Why is it she holds me to blame? Surely not for my quick bursts of bad temper. . . . *That* she will just have to get used to. She knows only too well how I love her. It can't be that. It must be something altogether different. She seems unable to settle down. She looks askance at everything she sees and nothing she hears finds favour with her. Yes, of course – that's it! She's been stuffed full of the wrong notions. Nursery nonsense. That accounts for the expression she assumes immediately there is talk about natural things, or when one attempts to show her something of life. So, it's a matter of getting her cured. Not to mince one's words, but speak straight from the shoulder about everything. It never fails – it is just what is needed. She's bright and as I concluded before, she is also fond of me. So, when the air has cleared, we'll be much closer and be able to live well together.

He took out a cigar and as he lit it, he asked: 'Have you been bored today, Aurora, or what is it that bothers you?'

Ory had her back towards Riber and her arms on the table. She was bent over a Norwegian newspaper, the contents of which she knew by heart, and did not look up when she answered: 'What kind of person is that Miss Sanna?'

'Oh, her,' said Riber in a voice full of contempt. He rose and paced a few times across the floor before he sat down again. 'I was just thinking about asking you what you thought about her,' he added.

'Well, I've never seen her before, but you have known

her a long time.'

'Yes, she's been with them a good few years and I have met her occasionally,' said Riber hesitatingly and seemingly absent-minded. 'By the way, I was once engaged to her,' he added resolutely, after a pause.

'Were you?' Ory lifted her head quickly, while her face gradually turned white. 'So, that was why. . . I couldn't imagine why,' she muttered the last bit to herself.

'She was very beautiful at that time,' continued Riber calmly. 'Well, she may be still, but I no longer notice it, she made too much trouble. She's a preposterous woman, believe me. We didn't suit each other at all.'

'Did she break off the engagement?' asked Ory, sounding as though she had to force out each word.

'Not at all. I did. I would gladly have paid a thousand pounds to get rid of her.'

'So, why did you get engaged?'

'Now, that's a question. . . . Ten minutes before it happened, I'd never thought about it.' He relapsed into thoughtfulness.

Ory, still with her back towards him, turned only her head to look at him.

'She'd got it into her head that she wanted me, you see,' continued Riber, 'and it's a funny business that. She was, as I've said, young and beautiful and didn't lack suitors. We men are easily affected when we get a little encouragement. We are not as capable of giving the cold shoulder as you lot are.'

'Are you telling me that it was out of pity you got engaged?' asked Ory with a hint of derision.

'I can't exactly claim that. I must have been, at least, a little in love with her, but it didn't last long. And that was entirely her own doing. I'll tell you what happened. Did you notice the scrofulous scar she had on her cheek? I told her once that scars like that had always repelled me. From that moment on, she wouldn't let me alone, she would have me, by hook or by crook, to kiss that scar. The ship was undergoing repairs at the time and I was here for quite a while. We were seeing each other daily and she would throw fits, entreat and beg me, weep and shout – God knows what she wouldn't do! But she never got me to do it!'

'It is strange that you wouldn't, when she was, after all, your fianceé,' said Ory with a slight quiver in her voice. Her face was still turned towards Riber, her expression tense and guarded.

'The more she carried on about it, the more impossible it became. The scar seemed, after a while, so revolting, that I almost retched each time I looked at it.'

'Was that when you broke off the engagement?'

'Yes. That's when I did it.'

'It seems a ridiculous reason for breaking off an engagement,' remarked Ory with the same unsteady voice.

'She would also have me say that filled teeth were prettier than healthy ones. If one loved a person who had some stoppings, one was not supposed to be able to stand healthy teeth. She was, to put it bluntly, an impossible creature.'

'Did it upset her?'

'Oh, Lord! She raved like a lunatic. Fortunately I was due to sail shortly afterwards. Yes, thank God, it went the way it did.' Riber sighed and shifted uneasily in his chair. 'It certainly was a case of luck being the better part of reason. That girl knew exactly what she wanted! She would come alone to my lodgings at any hour and naturally. . . .' Riber broke off his sentence and cleared his throat.

'Aren't you terribly sorry?' asked Ory formally.

'Hm . . . sorry?'

'Well, don't you know it is a terrible shame for a woman to have been engaged to someone and not to marry him. In your place I would have felt as though I had ruined her life.'

'Prejudice,' said Riber, shrugging it off.

'Is that what you call prejudice?' Ory turned her whole

body towards him.

'Yes, dearest. It is phrases that one uses until one believes in them, but then life itself teaches one something altogether different. To hear it advocated so vehemently by you, Ory, is almost comical, young and inexperienced as you are,' his voice was loving and his eyes smiled tolerantly.

'I can't bear you saying things like that!' exclaimed Ory and leapt up from her chair. 'It is . . . depraved,' she shielded her face with her hands and started to cry.

'But, my dear Ory,' Riber reached out his arm and pulled her to him by her dress. 'How can it hurt her when nobody knows? Well, it may disappoint her husband a little – if she ever gets one – but,'

'The Høsts know!' interrupted Ory, while she cried, 'and the others as well.'

'Only that we'd been engaged for a while – that was what he alluded to at the table, the ass – but they know nothing more. You are the first and only one I have ever told about it or will ever tell about it.'

Ory took her hands away from her face and looked uncomprehendingly at him.

'I felt I owed you that much, Ory,' continued Riber gently and patted her cheek. 'Be sensible and don't waste any more tears on it. Had the relationship had consequences, as they say, I might have understood you, but as it is – '

Emitting a dull sound like a suppressed scream, Ory knocked his hand away from her cheek and took some steps back. There she remained, staring at him with her hands stretched out in front of her and a look of horror on her face.

Riber opened his eyes wide and looked at a loss.

'What is there to be done with a child like this . . .' he muttered after a pause, leaning against the back of his chair with his arms crossed.

Ory ran over to the big horsehair sofa and threw herself headlong into it.

Some minutes passed. Then Riber rose and went over to where Ory lay and bent over her, as he put his hand on her neck.

'Don't touch me!' screamed Ory and pulled her head away violently. 'Go to her, to the other one, who has been your wife before me. You are *her* husband – not mine.'

'But, Ory, what kind of madness is this,' said Riber in a whining voice, as he straightened up and scratched his neck.

'Don't touch me ever again,' continued Ory, still provoked. 'If you do, I'll jump out of the nearest window, wherever we are, or I'll run away from you in the street – you may be sure of that . . .' she let her face, which she had lifted while she talked, fall heavily back onto the sofa.

Riber stood for a while looking at her. Her shoulders were shaking, but not a sound came from her.

He started walking up and down, from the window to the fireplace and past the sofa where Ory lay motionless.

A long time passed. Then he pulled a chair up to the sofa, sat down and started to talk in a low, unhappy voice:

'What good does it do to carry on like this, Ory? I knew very well that you were innocent and uninformed, but surely, you can't have expected a man of my age to enter the nuptial bed as pure as a vestal virgin? That doesn't happen in the *real world*, Aurora.'

He waited a little, but when Ory made no gesture in reply, he continued: 'Of course, men differ greatly. If only you knew the state of health some bridegrooms are in when they enter wedlock – but, obviously, you won't know anything of that. Thank God, I've always managed to stay clear of that sort of thing,' he cleared his throat thoroughly, 'apart from once, that is – accidents can happen to anybody, however careful – and it was incidentally a very mild case. I have a declaration from an excellent doctor, that it was quite all right for me to get married any time I wished.' Riber stammered and talked reluctantly. He had not really intended to let that out just then and he had a vague notion of it being a mistake, but something had driven him on, made him powerless and the words had slipped out.

'There is no reason for you to think, Ory, that I have lived a debauched life – far from it. My conduct has been better than most, I can safely say, better than anybody else that I've known about. Take Edvard Hals – isn't he just the sort of handsome, exemplary young man that any young girl would be glad to marry? If only you knew how he carried on. There was many a time we were together in a foreign port when I tried to advise him and even set him an example, but to no avail. No, dear – without bragging – I can honestly say that I've known where to draw the line. I have never, incidentally, touched a married woman and that even though I was once sorely tempted in that direction. But it was against my principles. I've always thought that if I didn't leave other men's wives alone, then God would punish me when I myself eventually got a wife. Now you can see, that even though I have knocked about a bit, I still have morals.' He had his arms lying on his knees and his head resting on them and the whole time he had talked he had been staring down onto the floor.

'Yes, you may well sigh, Aurora,' he said, when he heard faint groans from the sofa, 'When I really try hard to enter into your thoughts and concepts, I can in a way understand how you find this painful. But it's only a stage, my darling. When you are older and wiser you will look at things differently and see clearly that a man coming innocent into marriage is as much of a nuisance as a rarity.'

'Stop, stop!' Ory almost choked on the words.

'My darling Aurora, of course I shall,' he rose and went up close to the sofa. 'I felt it was my duty to instruct you in these matters and make this period of transition as easy as possible for you. Come on, Aurora, let me see you smile, as only you know how! Put your arms around my neck, give me a hug and show me that you have a heart as large as you are beautiful,' he put his arm round her waist and wanted to lift her up.

Ory let out a scream, got upon her knees and turned towards him. She was flailing in the air with her fists, and with her face contorted and her voice barely recognizable she cried out: 'I despise you!'

Riber, who had let go of her at once, tumbled backwards. His hands shook and a red line appeared across his forehead. His nostrils widened, only his lips remained still, although he looked as though he wanted to speak, but couldn't get out a word.

'So, that's the thanks I get for my openness,' he forced out after a while. His hands rose and fell heavily on Ory's shoulders, as he shook her hard in a senseless rage, while strange noises came from his open mouth. Ory's head lolled about above her slim throat. Her eyes were black as coals as she stared at him. Estranged and without fear she put up no resistance.

Riber was out of breath when he let go of her. He made a grab for his hat, which he slapped onto his head, pulled on his coat in such haste that the seams could be heard to burst, snatched up his cane and strode out of the house.

Ory stayed on her knees on the couch and gazed vacantly into space, while the final thud of the front door slamming rang in her ears. She felt as if she had been maimed by a deadly blow and her life was draining away imperceptibly from a rupture inside her.

'I have never, incidentally, touched a married woman. . . .' 'I have never, incidentally, touched a married woman . . .', the sentence was spinning in her head.

The best part of an hour went and Ory was still on her knees in the sofa, her arms hanging limply down and her eyes staring fixedly ahead.

There was a sudden crack from the table, as if someone had hit it with a fist. She gave a shout and shuddered, jumped off the sofa and ran towards the door, fumbling with the handle to open it. She quaked at the sight of the darkness outside and took a step backwards. With both hands pressed against her forehead she turned round carefully, throwing a timid glance over her shoulder at the table and then slowly letting her gaze wander all around the room.

Oh God, this is where she was . . . and out there was the boarding-house hallway and not her parents' bedroom as she had thought in her confusion.

Cramp-like spasms ran through her chest and the back of her head jumped in a series of twitches. She was on the verge of tears, but stifled them with her lips pressed hard together and her whole face contorted. She dared not cry; she had to be quiet, oh, so quiet, for that crack not to sound again.

She shut the door carefully behind her and in a couple of steps she was back by the sofa, where she sank down in despair.

No one in the world knew how unhappy she was. She gave way to her tears. Suddenly she felt enraged at Riber for having left her and not staying and suffering at seeing her in her misery.

At long last her tears dried up, while heaving sobs continued to shake her frame. Now she passed in review every word Riber had just uttered. It caused her intense pain.

And this man was her husband. Her husband for the rest of her life. What had she done – that she of all people should be punished by ending up with a man like that.

What a life he had led! Wallowing in dirt and vice and repulsive behaviour. And still he dared to claim that he was no exception and that there were those worse than him. The men she had known at home had never been like that – of that she was utterly convinced.

How many women, she wondered, had Riber had before her? Five, ten, twenty? How many . . . oh, how many . . . ? She wanted to know the exact number, each and every one of them. She was suddenly seized by a strong desire to know everything he'd ever done like that . . . every last detail. She would die if she couldn't know it all. Yes, she would examine and cross-examine him, make him tell her everything from beginning to end. It would be ghastly, but she would spare no effort, show no mercy for herself by leaving any stone unturned. She would go down, deep down into the filth and wallow in it too. A searing pang ripped into her and she felt relief only at the thought of the anguish she would endure.

She heard someone at the front door and rose quickly. Like lightning from a clear sky it became obvious to her that she would have to put on a brave face if she would have Riber talk. She rushed back to the sofa where she arranged herself to look asleep.

Even though her eyes were shut and her face pressed against her arms, which were resting on the side of the sofa, Ory still felt as if she could see everything. She noticed that Riber gave a start as he walked in and that he placed his hat carefully on the table. He then removed his coat and stuck his hands in his pockets as he approached the sofa. She felt his gaze burn its way into her neck and thought it would go on for ever.

'Aurora,' said Riber at last and touched her shoulder lightly. 'Won't you go to bed! It's almost four o'clock.'

'Aurora,' he repeated louder and shook her gently.

She lifted her face, which was pallid and unrecogniz-able, and looked timidly at him; but the light from the chandelier stung her eyes and she had to shut them again quickly.

'Aurora,' he said with a deep sigh. She could sense his agitation from the quiver in his voice. 'I was far too rash towards you. But you don't understand. . . . I don't know where I'm going, Aurora.'

'It was good of you to be honest with me.' Ory had to clear her throat to get any sound out at all. 'But I was horrified. . . . I had never imagined. . . . It is very painful.'

'Yes, Aurora, my love, my sweetest . . . it is painful. Is it very painful, Aurora?' he grabbed her in his arms and squeezed her impetuously.

'Just you give it some time and you'll see that it will get better,' continued Riber, suffused by tenderness. 'Be good to me, Aurora, please, be good to me ... I need it so much,' his head dropped onto her shoulder, while he implored her, whimpering like a sick child. 'I only have you in all the world, Aurora ... yes, that's how it has been ever since you came into my life. I'm nothing without you, nothing at all – I can only be something through you. And I have to learn bit by bit – there is a lot to learn. I have to learn to understand you and to see myself and everything else through your eyes, that I may think and feel the way you do. I want nothing more, Aurora, but you must understand it is completely alien to me – I have never thought particularly about these things, one way or another. I simply thought that it was supposed to be like that. Oh, but, Aurora, you can pull me across the abyss that separates us – my love gives you infinite power over me. You will see how I shall become virtuous and be worthy of you.' He clung onto her, his hands straying nervously away from her waist which he had been holding in a firm grip.

Ory was moved. She felt an urge to put her arms around his neck and kiss him, but then she could hear: 'I have, incidentally, never touched a married woman ...' and she had to restrain herself from pushing him away in disgust.

'I only want to make one condition,' she said in a voice hoarse from crying, 'and that is that you tell me *everything* about your past, every little detail.'

'Yes, Aurora. If that is what you want.'

'It is the only way I can get over it – the only thing that can bring me peace again. If you don't, I'll never get it off my mind.'

'You will get as complete a confession as is humanly possible, Aurora. But tonight we've both had enough. It can wait till a day we have good weather at sea. After all we're sailing tomorrow.'

· 7 ·

Their luggage was sent aboard and they had taken their leave of the landlady, whereupon Riber and Ory had gone out together to buy a few things before departure.

'Was there anything else then?' asked Riber, who carried the parcels, as they emerged from a shop in St Paul's Churchyard.

Ory stopped and thought. 'I can't remember anything else,' she said. 'But we're bound to have forgotten the most important item.'

'That outfit really suits you, Aurora,' Riber said, looking at Ory's dark blue outfit with a smile of approval. The tight-fitting coat was made of the same material as the dress and she was wearing a neat, little straw hat with a turned-up blue velvet lining, set off by a purple bird's wing. 'Those spotted veils certainly are flattering.'

'That's not why I wear one,' answered Ory and blushed. 'It keeps my hair in place even in a wind . . .'

'Oh, you little show-off!' Riber said teasingly and pulled out his watch. 'It's time we went and had some lunch. We can just about make it,' and they turned into an alleyway and arrived shortly after at a house, on which there was an enormous sign: Luncheon Rooms.

'It's not a particularly fancy place,' said Riber, 'but convenient for the moment.'

They walked up the steps and entered a large room, where people were eating and reading newspapers at the same time. It smelt of roast beef and grilled ham, mixed with tobacco. Waiters in jackets and white aprons confidently carried their trays on their fingertips moving deftly between the tables.

'Here,' said Riber and stopped by an empty table in the centre of the room, but just then somebody called out: 'Hallo, there my old friend!' and Captain Smith was there beside them.

'We have a corner all to ourselves,' said Smith. 'How about a "wee doch-an-dorris" and a chat before we go our ways?'

'Oh, dear,' thought Ory. 'How boring.'

'There's not a lot of time,' mumbled Riber grudgingly, as he and Ory followed Smith into a corner of the room, where Mrs Smith was sitting with a sizzling chop in front of her, in what seemed to be the smallest alcove in the room.

'How delightful that we should meet again,' exclaimed Mrs Smith. 'I spotted you first and asked my husband to invite you over here.'

'It's terribly hot in here,' remarked Ory and unbuttoned her coat, which Riber helped her out of.

'Did you enjoy yourself yesterday?' asked Mrs Smith, when Ory had taken a seat. 'They are nice people, but formal, don't you think?'

'Oh, I don't know. I've only just met them this once.'

'Oh, but they are formal. Most definitely. They have a gorgeous place though, which is nice to visit. It can't be bad to be rich. . . . But we sailors don't like all the formality – do we, Riber?'

'What will you have, Aurora?' asked Riber, engulfed by the menu.

'Do take the lamp chops,' recommended Mrs Smith. 'They are tender and juicy. That Miss Sanna is a real case, don't you think, Riber?'

'Well, now . . . ?' said Riber and looked questioningly at Ory.

'I'll have the lamb chops,' answered Ory.

'Yes, *do* ask Riber about Sanna,' remarked Smith, as he

took a sip from his port and winked cheekily. 'He knows her well enough.'

'Now that he's married and spoken for, as the saying goes, there can be no harm in that . . .' a greedy smile spread over Mrs Smith's face. 'I've been told that Riber really fancied her . . .'

Riber frowned. 'You are obviously a credulous person,' he said and looked coldly at Mrs Smith.

'Ha, ha, ha!' laughed Smith, 'Serves you right, miss la-di-da!'

'Yes, Riber always was one for a joke,' said Mrs Smith, while her smile faded from her mouth.

'Are we getting any food?' asked Ory, who was patting her hair nervously.

Riber gave their order to the waiter who had stood the whole time at the entrance to their alcove. He ordered roast beef for himself.

'You really ought to take the lamb chops,' said Mrs Smith. 'One gets bored by that interminable roast beef all the time, don't you think?'

'But don't you see,' Smith nudged Riber with his elbow, 'this man never has enough tender, young lamb's flesh to enjoy – eh?'

There was the sound of a loud smack, which made the two ladies jump. Mrs Smith looked up from her food and Ory rose startled. Smith sat open-mouthed and stared at Riber, while on his cheek white marks were showing against the red skin.

'So, you hit me, do you!' Smith burst out with an effort. 'You hit me. . . !' he repeated, as he jumped up from his chair and grabbed Riber by the throat.

'Calm down!' said Mrs Smith angrily and tugged at her husband's arm as hard as she could.

'The devil I will!' snarled Smith, whose hand Riber had calmly removed from his throat. He was about to make another grab at Riber, but his wife pulled him away.

'What is happening?' asked Ory, who had remained behind her chair, holding onto the back. She looked in amazement from one to the other and it struck her that maybe Riber had gone mad.

Riber laid his hand softly on hers. 'Don't worry about it, Aurora.' He looked embarrassed and unhappy and his cheeks were burning.

'If it's a fight you want, then come on . . .' Smith had wrested himself away from his wife and was about to pull off his coat.

'Listen – no more trouble!' Mrs Smith rose quickly and grabbed her husband around his wrists. 'Everybody knows how easy it is to trigger Riber off . . .' she continued with authority, 'although he's supposed to be better class than some of us. Just you show that you've had a better upbringing,' she straightened the collar on his coat, which had got rumpled. 'You should also learn to control your tongue a bit better, not always come out with your insinuations – you dirty old man.'

'I won't have it! I damn well won't have it,' thundered Smith, whose rage, all the same, seemed to be diminishing.

'No, of course not,' said Riber and threw a shy glance at Ory. 'You don't have to either, but let's not make a scandal here.'

'Why do *you* do it then?' asked Ory severely.

'I have never met such a bully,' exclaimed Smith, moving his neck about inside his collar, as if it had suddenly become too tight. 'And this is what they call refinement?!'

'Sit down and be quiet, Aurora,' said Riber.

'Yes, that goes for you too, my good man,' said Mrs Smith to her husband.

'I will, but only if Riber apologizes.'

The waiter arrived with the food and Riber started to eat at once.

'I suggest that we come to an understanding,' remarked Riber, 'and return to the matter another time.'

'Thank you very much!' said Smith with gruff irony.

Riber tapped on his glass.

'A bottle of Cliquot,' he demanded.

'Eat the rest of your food,' said Mrs Smith to her husband, as she again returned to her chops. 'Riber, I'm sure, will come up with an apology.'

Smith seemed appeased and started to eat with his eyes downcast, but a little while later his forehead swelled and his face flushed red.

Ory cut her chops into tiny little pieces, which she put slowly into her mouth, but still had trouble getting down. She brooded over what had happened and felt depressed by it.

The waiter brought the champagne in an icebucket, put a glass by each place and poured it out.

'I hope you will watch your tongue another time,' said Riber and wanted to clink glasses with Smith.

Smith grabbed his glass, looked at it for a moment, took a quick breath and threw its contents into Riber's face. A few seconds followed in absolute silence, while Mrs Smith and Ory watched Riber apprehensively. He was meticulously wiping his face with the serviette, after which he drained his own glass.

'Now we're quits,' said Smith, who watched Riber's every movement mistrustingly.

'Then we may as well drink to our reconciliation,' said Riber eventually in a friendly manner and filled his glass. 'Cheers!'

'Let *us* join in!' shouted Mrs Smith and all four toasted each other.

'And you mustn't mope any more now,' Smith nodded to Ory. 'Cheers. Mrs Riber.'

'That's right, Aurora. You love champagne, so drink now and you too, Mrs Smith.'

'Cheers, Mrs Riber,' nodded Mrs Smith. 'Bottoms up!' Both ladies emptied their glasses and Riber filled them up again.

'Let's have another bottle,' said Smith, when Riber had poured out the last drop. 'Allow me the pleasure.'

'That will have to wait until another time,' Riber

summoned the waiter and paid.

'You can't be in that much of a hurry,' was Mrs Smith's opinion. 'What's an hour more or less . . .'

'The tug is booked for three o'clock,' said Riber with a sudden edginess in his manner.

'Here's a man who knows how to wangle things,' exclaimed Smith. 'He's managed to line up for himself a cargo of general goods instead of ballast! As it is written: "To him that hath shall be given . . ." '

'Yes, we'll have a comfortable ship,' said Riber. 'As soon as we've cleared the Bay of Biscay we'll have the shutters off the rear windows and be sailing in summer sunshine. That's the least one can do, when one has a princess aboard,' he looked excitedly at Ory.

'All right then, it has been pleasant, despite our tiff,' said Smith. 'Have a good crossing and welcome to Pensacola – I'll remember the champagne.'

Back in the street they hailed a cab. Riber directed it to 'Victoria Docks' as they got in and the cab drove as fast as the throng of pedestrians and other vehicles permitted.

'Tell me now, what made you so angry,' said Ory, having to raise her voice to be heard above the din from the street.

'He talked indecorously.'

'About what?'

'About you.'

'About me? But you were talking about the food. . . .' Ory turned towards Riber and studied his face while she talked.

She suddenly gave a start. 'Oh, how disgusting!' she exclaimed and threw herself back into the seat, flushed bright red in the face.

'I would rather have been dead, than landed up in all this filth. Tell me one thing, did Mrs Smith understand?'

'I'm sure she did.'

'Then she has sunk that low. . . . Of course – she's been married a couple of years. I'll become like her as well. That will really suit you – are you looking forward to it?'

Ory was in despair. She moved about agitatedly in her
seat, buttoned and unbuttoned her coat with trembling
hands and her voice cut, sharp and penetrating, through
the noise outside.

Riber looked shattered.

'If only you had taken me with you and left and freed
me from those people's company,' continued Ory, more
and more irascible. 'They started immediately to harp on
about you and Sanna . . . don't come and tell me that
people don't know . . . , still you just sat there, drinking
toasts and buttering them up and getting me to do the
same. Oh, I feel sullied by it all.' She stamped her foot
and hid her face in her hands.

Riber let out a deep sigh. 'You are terribly severe, Ory,'
he said, as he moved up closer to her and pressed his lips
onto her neck, which was half turned towards him. 'But
all the same, I love you still and my longing for you pains
my heart. Oh, Aurora, you have to be mine a lot more
often,' he continued in a whisper, as he pulled her onto
his lap, turned her towards him and held her in a tight
embrace. 'I could squeeze you to death from love,' he
covered her face with insistent kisses.

'Let go of me,' shouted Ory, as she pushed her hands
against his chest and tore herself free with such a force
that she tumbled onto the opposite seat. There she took
up a posture of defiance, ready to parry with her fists. Her
chest heaved and she looked at her husband with fight in
her eyes.

Riber glanced at her. He looked weary and ashamed.

'Don't be angry with me, Aurora,' he said after a pause
and tried to grab her hand. Ory crossed her arms and
leaned further back in her seat.

'You've put me on too mean a ration,' he sighed. 'It
puts me under strain – no man can stand that sort of
thing.'

He lifted himself from the seat and went on his knees
before her. 'You can treat me how you like,' he turned his
blotchy face up to her. 'I'll be as faithful to you as a slave,

or even a dog. I swear it to you by our crucified Christ. Are you listening, Aurora?'

'Is it actually necessary to swear in that way?' thought Ory and shook her head perplexedly.

The cab stopped. Riber jumped to his feet, put on his hat, straightened his clothes, alighted and paid the driver.

Ory collected her parcels. Riber gave her his hand and she jumped down.

They walked in silence next to each other across the cobbled docks, that resembled a giant farmyard with enormous warehouses on three sides. The fourth side opened on to the water which was covered with large steamships and tall masted sailing ships, as many as there was room for lying against the quay, in the process of being either loaded or unloaded. The din from all the activity reverberated all around.

'Stop, Aurora! Here she is. *Orion* ahoy!'

'Ahoy!' was returned and a freckled man with a flat cap and a woollen scarf greeted them from the railing of a full-rigged ship.

'What the devil have you done with the gangway, mate?' asked Riber.

'Captain's orders were to have the ship ready at three – precisely,' answered the mate and nodded his head adamantly as he talked. With his obstinate nose and the scraggy bit of beard under his chin he resembled a goat.

'You are an ass, mate! You knew that my wife was coming aboard.'

'I thought that madam could make do with the ladder.'

'So, that's what you thought – was it,' scoffed Riber. 'Give me the parcels and see if you can manage, Aurora.'

Ory grabbed the handrails that were hanging loosely down along either side of the rope-ladder and climbed agilely up to the hammock net, where the mate reached out his hand and pulled her aboard.

'Welcome, madam.'

'Thank you,' said Ory and looked about on the

spacious deck, which was wet and dirty, with coal spilt here and there.

'What kind of a deck is this?' asked Riber, as he jumped across the rail. 'It looks like a pigsty!'

'Can't do more than one thing at a time, cap'n. The coal and the water have just come aboard.'

'It hasn't even been cleaned behind here,' Riber carried on, pointing at some sacks and baskets with live chickens, which were piled on top of each other near the companion hatch and almost hiding it.

'We haven't finished hauling away yet,' answered the mate unabashed.

'What the hell are you up to?' Riber stamped his foot. 'All hands on deck!' he shouted afterwards.

'Would you like to go to the cabin, Aurora. Here you will only be in the way!'

Ory who had moved a little away, was looking at the turbid water in the harbour, where the ships lay moored to buoys. Distracted by the noise of work going on around her she didn't hear what was said to her.

Riber was about to approach her, but just then the mate who was going in the opposite direction shouted to him: 'The chronometer hasn't arrived, cap'n!'

'Mate!' Riber screamed piercingly and made Ory jump.

The mate came aft.

'Have you a screw loose, or have you planned to shipwreck us, as you want us to sail without a chronometer?' asked Riber furiously.

'I had to wait to see if it would come or not. I went to see the watchmaker last night and told him we had to be out of the dock by twelve o'clock.'

'At twelve! Do you think the watchmaker, living as close as he does to the docks, doesn't know what time the high tide is? But that's just like you, you lie when you ought to tell the truth and always tell the truth when you ought to lie.'

'I did tell him three o'clock just before I left though,' put the mate in quickly and with a brilliant smile. 'So it can't be my fault.'

'You deserve a flogging,' Riber advanced a step toward the mate with his hand raised.

At that moment, Ory, who had joined them, grabbed Riber by the arm and looked pleadingly at him.

As if by magic, Riber's expression changed in a flash, the tension caused by his anger was resolved and his features became mild and compliant. A sensation, that was half emotion, half wonder, ran through Ory and the consciousness of her own worth and power caused her a sudden thrill.

'There is no need for madam to worry,' said the mate with an icy smile. 'The captain would never lay his hand on his mate, Anton Marius Bruvig.'

'Have you finished preaching!' Riber turned to the mate again, as he took Ory by the hand and pulled her a little to himself, as if to shield her. 'Make them stop the hauling, damn it, so that I can get ashore.'

The mate shouted down to the people on the quay that they should stop hauling. But as the ship was already pulling away a gangplank was put from the railing to the quayside.

'Make yourself as comfortable as you can, Aurora,' Riber squeezed her hand. 'I'll follow by rail.'

'Shall we wait for you, captain?' shouted the mate when Riber had got ashore.

'Are you out of your mind! Get down to Gravesend as quickly as you can.'

· 8 ·

Ory went down the steps, which descended in a curve into the gloomy forecabin that was used as a messroom. In the middle was a long table, covered with a waxed table cloth; and on both sides were long benches with high backs. To the left a door was open into the pantry, where mugs and pots were hung from the ceiling, completely covering it. The cabin did not seem particularly clean and it smelt unpleasantly of smoke.

Ory tied the handle of the door leading into the aft cabin, but after tinkering with it unsuccessfully, she gave it up.

She sat down on one of the benches in the forecabin and stared sadly in front of her. Noise from on deck was reaching down to her. Voices of the men singing while they lumbered round the capstan, interrupted occasionally by a blaring shout of command from the mate.

The door to the aft cabin slid open into the wall beside it and a big, sixteen-year-old boy with smooth, fair hair and a fat, snub nose appeared, snorting and rubbing his eyes. He wore a blue, cotton shirt and canvas trousers that had once been white.

'I couldn't get the door opened,' said Ory and rose. 'Show me how to do it.'

The boy removed his hands from his soot-covered face and looked in amazement at Ory.

'It's simple,' he said and pulled the door in its groove in the wall. 'It's a sliding door.'

'But . . . it's Halfdan!' exclaimed Ory. 'Fancy that . . . I didn't recognize you until you talked.'

'Is the captain aboard as well?'

'He was, but he had to leave again. Why are you crying?'

'I'm not crying, it's the smoke.'

'Why are you so dirty?' she regarded him with reluctant sympathy.

Halfdan glanced at his filthy shirt sleeves and let his gaze continue to wander over his trousers. 'I don't think I'm particularly dirty,' he said complacently.

'It is terrible. How often do you change?'

'Once a week. This was clean on yesterday. It's easy to get mucky on a ship.'

'I promised your mother that I would keep an eye on you. I've also got a parcel for you and lots of greetings, of course. And I was told to find out if you hadn't regretted going to sea?'

'Not in the slightest.' Halfdan cocked his head, but the tone of his voice was not particularly convincing, thought Ory.

She shook her head doubtfully.

'But I'm forgetting – I haven't congratulated you on your wedding,' said Halfdan. 'They wrote from home telling me that it would be a year or so before we got a mistress on board the *Orion*, but they can't have reckoned on the autocrat.'

'The autocrat?' said Ory astonished.

'Crikey,' said the boy and bit his finger. 'How am I to remember that you've become his wife? . . .'

'Do you call him the autocrat?'

'Yes, and not only us on board, but every sailor in Norway. But don't tell him, Ory. He's capable of throwing me overboard.'

'The autocrat,' said Ory musingly. 'There is nothing insulting in that name.'

'No, more like the opposite. It's another name they have for the Russian tsars.'

'Has the luggage come on board?'

'Yes, this morning.'

'Where is it?'

'In the captain's cabin. Come on, I'll show you.' He pulled the door open and let Ory go in first, but she had barely gone beyond the doorstep, when she turned sharply round and almost knocked Halfdan off his feet in her haste to get out.

'What terrible smoke,' she said and gasped for air. 'Does it always act up like that?'

'It's the first time it's been lit. I was given the order to make everything nice for when the missus arrived.'

'Go in there and put it out, Halfdan, and open everything you possibly can. Just see how the smoke is pouring out of there – I'd much rather sit in the cold.'

Halfdan got a bucket of water from the pantry and poured the whole lot into the fat-bellied copper stove. Ory could hear an angry hissing.

'Cor,' said Halfdan and scratched his head. 'There's a fine bit o' work I've landed meself up with.'

'You used too much,' said Ory, who had been watching him from the doorway. 'A few splashes would have done it.'

Halfdan shook his head and contemplated the thick, black water, which oozed down the legs of the stove and along the floor.

'Yes – too much or too little spoils everything,' he said despondently. 'But what good does that do? I'll have to go and fetch a bucket of water and a swab,' he folded back his shirt sleeves to above the elbows.

'I'm going up for a bit,' said Ory. 'Make sure that you air the cabin well, Halfdan.'

When Ory came up on deck, the ship had moved a fair bit away from the quay and ahead of her bow was a small, squat tug. From its funnel rose a thick pillar of black smoke, dispersed by the light wind a short way up and drifting in big light puffs in between the *Orion*'s masts. From the stern of the tug an Englishman was shouting something in a hoarse voice towards the *Orion*.

'Man at the helm!' commanded the mate. 'Stand by at the cables!'

The crew ran to and fro. As each one of them passed Ory, who stood by the companion hatch, they briefly lifted their caps.

'Steamer ahoy!' somebody roared from the *Orion*'s fo'c'sle.

'Hello!' came an answer back from the tug. At the same time a dark object flew through the air above the *Orion*'s bowsprit and fell with a thud onto the deck of the tug.

There was a great deal of noise passing like an echo between the two and the tug turned round in a half-circle. Shortly afterwards, a jerk could be felt as the *Orion* started moving behind the other vessel at no more than twenty yards distance. They glided slowly between the berthed ships.

We're being towed, realized Ory, who had been watching with great interest. But how were they going to get out? There was a stone wall straight ahead.

On reaching the end of the dock suddenly, as if by magic, an opening appeared in the wall. It extended quickly and became a wide gap, through which they sailed proudly into a large, square basin. Another stone wall at the other end opened in the same way and then they were out in muddy, grey water, with frothy, little waves, that teemed with ships of all shapes and sizes. Steamers and sailing ships, huge hulks, heavily loaded, some with broken masts and gunwales, pulled by tugs, went side by side with fast, elegant pleasure yachts that were passing swiftly along as though they were taking part in a race, with music aboard and garlands of flags flapping in the rigging.

'Is this the Thames?' Ory asked a sailor who passed her.

'Yes, madam.'

Ory was captivated by this impressive new world that had revealed itself so suddenly to her.

If only the air had been less dense and impenetrable.

But the factory chimneys along the banks, as well as the steamers, were spewing out masses of suffocating smoke, which stung one's eyes and left a taste of sulphur in one's mouth.

Then occasionally there would be a clear patch and she could see windmills on the shore and enormously long buildings, which assumed fantastic shapes in the haze.

Further down they came closer to the shore, which by then consisted of long stretches of mud-flats.

'Will madam, please, move over a little. We're going to wash down the deck.'

Ory, who had rested her arms on the hammock netting and had her chin resting in her hands, turned round, nodded to the mate and went further aft.

A moment later she was again asked to move and she withdrew to the stern. But even there a deckhand emptied a bucket of water just in front of her, with a: 'Watch out!' before he started to scrub.

Ory looked round her. Streams of water were flowing everywhere and all over the deck men were scrubbing.

She supposed she had better go below. But what a pity! Just now, when all the ships were beginning to light their lanterns, it would have been such fun to stay.

She lifted her dress with both hands and walked on tiptoe along to the companion hatch, which was held open for her by the mate, as he commented: 'Madam's footwear, I dare say, was not intended for the wet.'

Below in the cabin it was half dark and cold and the acrid smell of smoke still filled the air.

Ory sat down on the edge of the day-bed and looked at the bare walls, where the white panelling glowed in the waning light. In front of the sofa was a large, oval mahogany table. It must have been freshly polished, as its surface reflected the lamp hanging down from the skylight.

The stern windows had hatches on, hence that part of the cabin was almost in total darkness. Ory perceived them as mirrors glinting from their deep recesses between the sloping stern timbers. What seemed like enormously large window-sills joined to a long bench round the stern post and were covered with fitted leather cushions. It suddenly struck Ory that it was there the ghost of Riber's father must have appeared that night in the Channel. She shuddered and her gaze roamed about uneasily. What was *that* over there in the corner? Two glowing eyes stared at her from below a tall, thin hat. She went cold from fear. Now she could see it more clearly; a dwarf sat on his haunches with a fat belly sticking out from between his legs.

'Halfdan!' shouted Ory, as she rushed towards the door and jerked at the handle, which would not obey. 'Halfdan,' she repeated plaintively, but at last the door opened and she ran into the forecabin.

Just then the hatch door opened and somebody came downstairs.

'Is it you, Halfdan?'

'Yes.'

'Where have you been all this time?'

'Polishing knives in the galley, of course.'

'There is something sitting on its haunches inside the cabin,' said Ory in a whisper, as she followed close behind Halfdan into the pantry.

'Something you're imagining I suppose.'

'Then go and have a look for yourself, if you dare.'

'Trust me!' Halfdan stalked noisily into the cabin, but added: 'You'd better come along and show me.'

'There,' said Ory and pointed from the door, where she had remained standing.

'It's the stove,' exclaimed Halfdan and both of them burst into hearty laughter.

'Could you show me where everything is down here,' said Ory when Halfdan had lit the lamp. 'Is that where the captain sleeps?' She pointed to a curtain a short distance from the day-bed.

'Yes,' said Halfdan. 'I'll go in there and light the lamp.'

'Are there no other cabins?' asked Ory who had followed him in.

'No.'

'None at all?'

'Apart from the pantry and the breadroom next to the saloon, no.'

'Listen, what's that?' A muffled, grating rattle could be heard.

'That was the anchor going down. Now we're in Gravesend.'

'Are we going to stay here?'

'Yes, at least until the captain comes. Tomorrow morning we'll be weighing anchor. But now it's time for me to go up and make tea.'

'Do you always have an early supper?'

'Yes, seven or thereabouts. When we're sailing it's even earlier.'

When Halfdan had left, Ory looked all around the sleeping quarters. The floor was covered in linoleum checkered in large grey and red squares, similar to that in the saloon. A high bed was built into the main wall with three rows of drawers underneath and a canopy up top, from where hung dark green, cotton curtains with a white print, flowery pattern. Against the end wall, near the bed, was an oak washstand with a lid and a tall, slim chest of drawers. A long, narrow chest stood against the wall opposite the bed. Ory opened the lid and saw that it was full of rolled up charts. In the fourth wall was the curtain-covered entrance and next to that a white painted cupboard with a flap in the middle and drawers on top and at the bottom. Just behind the head of the bed Ory noticed a narrow door. She turned the key and opened it. Inside was a small, square room with hooks in the ceiling from which hung coats, trousers and a couple of handweights attached to the ends of a rope.

Ory stretched on tip-toe to find out how wide the bed was. There were no sheets on it and only one pillow on top of the bolster. She sighed and grew thoughtful.

Had anybody else lain next to Riber in that bed? Sanna, perhaps. She had obviously visited him aboard. Or could it have been any of the many others? It obsessed her again, this nagging desire to know everything about him.

It may have sounded worse than it actually was. Riber was after all prone to exaggeration. He may have made himself look worse than he really was.

'I have, incidentally, never touched a married woman.'

If only he had not said those words! As if he had wanted full marks for good behaviour and had expected nobody ever to object to him having touched any other women.

But still, it might not be that bad. . . . If only it was a little, a tiny bit better rather than worse, then she would try to love him and forget it.

Better than worse? What would be the worse? The notion was not so clear, but when he had told everything, she would know . . .

If it was true what Riber had said, that the majority were worse than he was, how could mothers then want their daughters married? Like her own mother – how satisfied she had been with the engagement!

She removed her hat and sat down on the chart box, her head in her hands. From the forecabin she could hear the officers' small talk as they ate.

This, then, was going to be her home for at least a year. The saloon during the day and squeezed up in this narrow bed at night. If only she would be allowed to sleep on the outside, then she could get up when Riber had gone to sleep and lie down on the day-bed in the saloon, or on the leather cushions on the window-ledges, which were each as long and as wide as this bed.

Dear, oh, dear! It might not be as bad after all. To sail along to foreign shores, to a totally different part of the world, where it was summer all year round, that *would* be fun. And then she had Halfdan – that at least was something familiar.

The men looked kind. She would make a point of being friendly with them. Wish them a good morning every day when she first went on deck. It was nice to be the Captain's wife aboard a ship like the *Orion*.

Wondering what time it was, she buttoned up her coat to fetch her pocket watch, but noticed in the same instant a clock set in an octagonal frame of brown wood, built into the wall.

Nine already and Riber still not aboard. By train he should have been in Gravesend hours ago.

Halfdan appeared at the door. 'Shall I stay up and wait with the tea till the captain arrives?' he asked.

'Do you usually do that?'

'No,' said Halfdan reluctantly. 'Usually when we're in foreign ports, the captain doesn't have supper aboard. He always comes back too late.'

'Does he always come late?'

'All captains do. Would you like to eat now? I've laid the table in the salon.'

'Yes, thank you, I'll have some food.'

Ory went into the cabin and sat down by the table. It was laid with white bread and biscuits, butter in a round porcelain dish, salt meat, anchovies and a glass cheese dish with a whole Dutch Edam. The sugar bowl of white porcelain with gold embossed edges had a lug missing and the cream jug was without a handle.

'Sit down and have a bite with me,' said Ory, when Halfdan had poured the tea.

'Thank you, but I have already eaten,' said Halfdan and sat down at the end of the bench.

'It doesn't matter – come on . . .'

'I can't, I'm chewing tobacco.'

'You – chewing tobacco!' Ory cried and dropped her hand, still holding a piece of bread.

'So what?'

'But, Halfdan! What if I wrote home about it . . .'

'Do you imagine *I* would worry about that!'

'I'm going to see that you break that habit,' said Ory decisively, 'just you wait and see.'

'Why are you staring at me?' asked Ory after a pause.

'I've just remembered something,' answered Halfdan, recollecting himself.

'Tell me . . .'

'If you promise not to get angry.'

'Why should I get angry? Say it . . .'

'You *will* get angry, but if you absolutely want me to. . . . It was at the time when we were taking dancing lessons . . . do you remember? I had made a bet with some boys that I would kiss you, with them looking on.'

'I've never heard such impertinence!' exclaimed Ory indignantly. 'Had it been Gina Bekkevold I could have understood it – but me!'

'The whole point was that it had to be you,' said Halfdan, a pale shade of red spreading over his face. 'Otherwise there would have been no reason for the bet.'

'At least you lost the bet,' said Ory triumphantly.

'I prepared myself to do it twice, but I didn't have the pluck.'

'I dare say,' said Ory sarcastically, as she folded her napkin. Halfdan rose to clear the table. 'Even so, I regret now that I didn't do it,' he said with a beguiling smile.

'What was that you said?!' Ory looked crushingly at him, but Halfdan pretended not to notice.

'What did you say?!' repeated Ory, with a frown, while she stared fixedly at him.

Halfdan continued calmly gathering the things onto the tray. But at last he could not help himself and looked up at Ory, whose offended expression appeared so comical that he could hardly suppress his laughter. At the same moment Ory's expression softened, the corners of her mouth vibrated and suddenly they both exploded with laughter.

After that Ory went into the sleeping quarters and started to arrange her clothes in a drawer. Halfdan had pulled out the right one in the tall, slim chest before he had said good night.

To find room for her boots, she squatted down in front

of the drawers beneath the bed and started to pull out one of the long, heavy drawers by its handles. Just then something dark and sharp sprang up from one of the corners and in a split second a large rat had run across Ory's hand and onto the floor, where she heard its paws pattering across the linoleum like the sound of hailstones.

Stupefied by fear, Ory had fallen backwards, but caught herself with her hand against the floor. She jumped up with a hollow, stifled cry and ran senseless with fear into the saloon, up onto the day-bed and from there onto the table, where she curled up with her skirts wrapped tightly around her legs.

She did not dare to move, or lose sight of the floor for one moment, for fear that the rat would come up to her. With frightened wide-open eyes, she kept up an incessant watch on all sides. Sometimes she seemed to hear something moving about in a corner that startled her and made her heart miss a beat. Miss Thorsen had always said that evil people were born again as rats and an old priest she had once asked about it had said that it was not impossible.

Ory was certain that this was a fact. Why else would she have this insane fear of rats? Throughout her life, every time she had seen one, her blood had curdled.

She could no longer stand this huddled position. She bent forward slowly, onto her knees and rested her hands on the table.

If only Riber would come. It must have been at least eleven o'clock. Where had he got to?

What if something had happened to him – there were often accidents on the railway. Or he might have fallen into the water as he was coming aboard. Maybe she had become a widow this evening. Maybe she had been one for many hours, or maybe she had become one just a moment ago. . . .

If that was the case she would have to spend the whole night like this on the table, until Halfdan arrived to do the tidying up in the morning. How could she stand it? She shivered with cold, her knees hurt and she had pains in her chest from tiredness.

Suddenly she heard a shout from on deck and the sound of someone running. She listened tensely for some minutes. Then steps approached the skylight – irregular, faltering steps, she thought. It could not be Riber, he never walked like that.

Shortly afterwards, somebody stumbled on the stairs and came rushing down like an avalanche and landed with a thud; and there was a loud noise of something hard hitting the floor, followed by absolute silence.

Ory felt her blood pounding in her temples and her ears were ringing. She felt she would die of fright.

A little later, fumbling movements started up again. Whoever it was crawled about on the floor and managed to get up and over to the door, groping about for the handle.

Ory was looking breathlessly over her shoulder at the door, which at long last slid open and let in Riber, without a hat and with a pale face. Under his arm he carried a tall, square box.

'Oh dear, it's only you!' cried Ory, and gave vent to her fear with loud sobs.

Riber drew back in surprise. 'I didn't see you,' he said in a strangely dull voice and put a hand up to his forehead.

'There is a rat in here,' sobbed Ory. 'A large, terrible rat.'

'A rat,' snorted Riber and seemed not to understand.

'It jumped out of the drawer under the bed, when I wanted to put away my boots. Take me, carry me up on deck! I want to go ashore!' Crawling round the table on her knees, she had turned towards Riber and was stretching her hands towards him.

'Quiet, child, be quiet,' said Riber with the same dull voice and waved dismissively with his hand. 'I fell down the stairs – just like that. That blasted Halfdan – why didn't he leave the lamp on.' He sat the box down on the bench at the stern and felt along his legs, as though to reassure himself that his limbs were still in one piece.

'Won't you lift me up! Please, lift me up,' continued Ory whimpering.

Riber opened the lid of the box, bent over it and listened.

'Magnificent chronometer,' he mumbled. 'No damage done.' Then he turned round and looked at Ory with sheer surprise on his face, as if he'd only just seen her.

'Well, look at her,' he exclaimed with a foolish smile, straightening himself up and snapping his fingers. 'The silly-billy is sitting on top of the table,' he walked over to Ory and threw his arms about her.

'Didn't you hear what I told you – that there is a rat in here!' shouted Ory, as she grabbed him by the shoulders and shook with all her might. Just then she became aware of a strong smell of wine on his breath and let go of him instantly. 'Oh, my God, my God! What am I to do. . . . I'm dying of fright,' she let her elbows fall onto the table and hid her face in her hands.

'Did you say you would die, Aurora, then let me die for you!' Riber straightened his back and thumped his chest pathetically.

'The rat,' groaned Ory, 'the rat.'

'What kind of rat is it you are talking about, Aurora?' Ory raised her head and grabbed hold of him. 'Haven't you listened to anything I've said!' she shouted desperately, as if to someone deaf, but looked at the same time imploringly into his face.

'Just show me where it is,' said Riber and unbuttoned his coat. 'I'll make short work of it.' He grabbed the poker and whirled it round his head before he dropped down on the floor, where he rattled it about everywhere, making as much noise as possible.

Ory was standing on the table with her skirt tucked well between her legs, watching intently.

Suddenly she shouted: 'There it is! It's run into the forecabin. For God's sake, Riber! Shut the door – quick!'

Riber, panting from the exertion, got up and pulled the door to.

'Whew,' he said, wiping his forehead with a handkerchief.

'Dear God in Heaven, please, don't let there be any more,' prayed Ory with folded hands and was about to step from the table onto the day-bed, when Riber grabbed her round the waist and lifted her down.

'My sweet pet,' he said without letting go and his face drew close to hers. 'Kiss me and let's go to bed.'

'Ugh, no – you've been drinking,' said Ory and pushed him away so abruptly that he tumbled against the wall. 'You look so different and your voice is unrecognizable.'

Riber's face fell and he sighed. 'Yes, Aurora, I've been drinking,' he said with a slurred voice after a while. 'It's not a habit, though – it happened purely by accident. I ran into some old friends.'

'So, that's why I had to wait all this time.'

'Have you missed me, Aurora?' Riber opened his arms wide.

Ory turned her back on him, walked across to the bench and sat down.

Riber followed. He grabbed her hand, pulled at her and all of a sudden pushed his fingers down into the collar of her dress.

'You're strangling me!' screamed Ory and tore away his hand.

'Strangling you . . .' repeated Riber in a voice that seemed to fail him, whereupon he folded his arms across his chest. He became thoughtful and swayed to and fro.

'So now she believes I want to strangle her,' he continued a little later. 'She, whom I love more than anything in the world, even more than my own life.' He frowned and for an instant his face quivered.

'Don't be a fool,' said Ory angrily.

'No,' answered Riber, 'I won't be a fool. Christ was crucified to save all human beings. What good is saving those one doesn't know and don't concern one. . . .

What's more, it's futile. It's only possible to save one in a lifetime.'

'At least you oughtn't to blaspheme because you are drunk,' said Ory.

'I'm wondering about something,' Riber stroked his eyebrows with one of his fingers. 'Tell me honestly, Aurora: would you rather be rid of me?'

'The way you are tonight, yes, I'd rather be rid of you.'

'Rather be rid of you . . .' repeated Riber and looked dreamlike into the air. Then he went into the sleeping quarters.

Ory leaned back against the sloping stern and shut her eyes. She was about to collapse from exhaustion. The previous night she had hardly slept at all. If only Riber would go to bed and leave her alone.

A squeaking sound issued from the chamber, followed by a click. It must have been the flap in the cupboard he had opened. If only he would settle down quietly.

Soon after Riber was back, carrying something in his hand, that he hid behind a fold in his coat. He positioned himself with deliberation in front of Ory and said: 'Aurora, my wife, my love, look at me. Here I am: Carl Adolph Riber, thirty-two-years-old, son of good parents and holding a good position. My only misfortune is that I have you as a wife.'

'That's entirely your own doing,' mumbled Ory spitefully.

'Yes, of course, my own doing entirely. But when I now shoot myself, it is not for my own sake, but for yours, that you may be rid of me, as you've said you want to be and to let you have a chance to be happy with someone else. Please, kiss me goodbye,' he reached out his hand towards her.

'You might try sleeping it off first,' said Ory, shifting uncomfortably on the bench. 'You're talking nonsense.'

'You refuse even to kiss me,' cried Riber in an altered, high-pitched voice. 'Do you know what I ought to do?' He grabbed her roughly by the arm and pulled her up towards him. 'I should beat the living daylights out of you – shouldn't I?'

'Let go of me,' said Ory, incensed, and tried to twist out of his grasp.

'Or even better – I could shoot you!' he raised his hand and something glimmered. 'Who could stop me, may I ask?'

'Go ahead – shoot,' she said, looking obstinately into his eyes. 'But won't you, please, let go of my arm first?'

'Do you see this?' Riber held a pistol close up to Ory's eyes. 'Get down on your knees and beg for your dear life, which you are about to lose.'

'Nonsense,' said Ory, vexed, and hit away the hand that held the gun.

'Yes, Aurora, it is nonsense,' his voice had changed again. Now it was tender and humble. 'I cannot harm you, but if you want me to, I'll shoot myself – as surely as you see me standing here with the pistol in my hand. One little word and you are at liberty forever. But you have to tell me that that is what you want – I won't kill myself for nothing.'

Ory, leaning back on the bench, raised her eyebrows in an expression of indifference.

'Answer me, Aurora: Yes or no?'

'Won't you stop this comedy,' said Ory impatiently. 'I am tired and weary and I'm going to go to pieces.'

'I want an answer,' shouted Riber and stamped his foot. 'Yes or no?'

'Shoot, by all means.'

'It is yes then?'

'Yes, go ahead.'

'Good,' Riber's face, which had been red and excited, suddenly drained and assumed a deathly grey pallor. From his throat came a sound as if he was swallowing something with great difficulty. He raised the gun and placed it against his temple.

In a flash it occurred to Ory that the weapon might be loaded. She shot up and hit the pistol out of Riber's hand.

His hand sank down, numbed. . . .

'Do you want to frighten the life out of me?' exclaimed Ory and burst into tears. 'You ought to be ashamed of yourself, the way you behave towards me.'

'No, Aurora, I want to be good to you,' said Riber, and it struck Ory that he had become quite sober. 'I thank you for giving me life, that must mean that somewhere in you there is a spark of love for me.' The words were pronounced in jerks and barely audible, while his face dissolved into tears. He slumped down on the bench shielding his eyes with his hand.

'Tell me,' whispered Ory, as she laid her arm across his shoulders and bent over him: 'Was the pistol loaded?'

'Look for yourself.'

Ory kissed him.

Riber shut his eyes and let his face fall onto her shoulder. 'Let me rest here for ever,' he said, 'there is nowhere else I can be at peace.'

It was blowing up fiercely from the south-west. Riber
stood aft on the pitching deck, holding on to the edge of
the companion hatch, while he sometimes squinted up at
the black sky, broken occasionally by a dirty yellow drift
of clouds passing by. Mid-watch had just started, the
close-reefed upper topsails had been furled and the *Orion*
was now carrying only her lower topsails. They had cleared
the Channel in the afternoon, the whole time having to
tack against the wind. When they entered the Bay of
Biscay they met with choppy water and a heavy
groundswell that came from no one direction and the
wind had also increased.

The mate approached the hatch and took a hold of the
door handle.

'She's never rolled this bloody much before,' said Riber,
annoyed. 'But that's what one gets for not being present
to look after everything oneself. You have obviously put
all the light stuff at the bottom and the heavy goods on
top.'

'We stored everything in the order it arrived, cap'n.'

'How convenient for you! And why do you think mates
are hired?'

'I presume it's because skippers can't do without them,'
said the mate drily. 'Aye, aye!'

The ship plunged her nose into the sea, the mate
crouched and hung on tight.

'Had you only been as quick in the head and with your

as you are sharp with your tongue, Mr Mate . . .' a
wer of foam swallowed the rest of Riber's words.

'The devil's own mouth that fellow has,' snarled Riber,
as the mate disappeared through the hatch way and
pulled it shut behind him with a loud bang.

'Who's at the helm?' Riber called out, as he swayed
with the movement of the ship to keep his balance on his
way across to the wheelhouse.

'Zacharias, cap'n.'

'What's the pointing?'

'Sou'west to west, cap'n.'

'Second mate, ahoy!'

'Ahoy, cap'n!' came the answer and a tall, thin man
wearing a souwester pulled well down over his ears and
with something bulky wound many times round his neck,
appeared in the circle of light thrown on to the deck by
the compass light and the glow from the skylight.

'Cover the skylight with the tarpaulin,' Riber ordered,
'and set the fore topmast stay'sail!'

'Aye, aye, cap'n.'

'If anything untoward happens – tell me. I'm going
below for a bit. In an hour's time we're changing course.'

'Aye, aye, cap'n.'

Riber went below. The lit lamps were tossing about,
oozing out smoke.

In the saloon he took a rolled up chart that was lying
on the day-bed and smoothed it out across the table,
where he bent over and held it and himself in place by
clamping it down with his arms. He braced his straddled
legs, in tall sea-boots, against the moving floor, studying
the chart and measuring it with compass and ruler.
Occasionally he would mutter to himself and nod with
satisfaction. Then he rolled up the chart and put it back
on the day-bed, whereupon he went into his sleeping
quarters and approached the bed, fastening the flapping
curtains on either side.

'This is great fun!' cried Ory. 'The cabin seems to have
come alive and decided to have fun and games. And all

the strange noises it's making from its efforts; breathing, panting and groaning.'

'So you are lying here awake, you naughty child,' Riber poked his head in under the draped curtains and kissed her.

'You are all wet,' said Ory and wiped her mouth with the sheet; she had raised herself up on one elbow.

'It's this thing which has taken in a bit of spray,' said Riber, removing the woolly hat from his head and throwing it on the floor. He pulled off his reefer as well, stuck his arm under Ory's neck and started kissing her until half his body was inside the bed.

'You are jolting me! It hurts!'

'It's the pitching and tossing . . . you should feel my knees every time they are thrown against the edge of the bed.'

'Is the weather very bad?' asked Ory.

'There's a bit of a wind. But what does it matter, as long as it doesn't upset my pet at all.'

'No, I'm rather enjoying it,' said Ory cheerfully. 'Just looking at the way those clothes throw themselves off the wall only to be splattered back in place, makes me laugh. A little while ago your weights came tumbling out of the cupboard – they sounded like a whole canon charge.'

'You are wonderful, Ory! What a great waste it would have been if you hadn't become a sailor's wife. No seasickness, no nonsense, it's as though you were born and bred aboard ship.'

'Are you going back up?'

'Just for a short while,' said Riber, having put his reefer back on. 'I won't go to bed before we've changed course.'

'You should have seen my clothes, that I'd put down on the suitcase,' giggled Ory. 'They jumped right up into the bed with me and I had to get up and put them in a drawer.'

'Be careful, Aurora, you could easily come to harm down here.'

'I did fall too,' said Ory with satisfaction. 'And I hurt

my knees and hands quite a bit, but I just laughed it off. Here she goes again!' The large brass tacked wooden chest slid across the floor and charged into the chart box.

'What the Devil . . . ?' said Riber. 'I mean to say . . . that thing there should have been tied down long ago. I'll go and turn out Halfdan and send him down here. You just go back to sleep!'

Sleep! Easier said than done – had the motion at least come from only one direction, but she was being bounced and jolted all over the place. Sometimes the head of the bed would lift up, until she was almost standing and when it had gone back, the same thing would happen at the foot end and she had to hold on for dear life or end up doing a backward somersault.

What was that noise there? Ory raised herself above the edge of the bed and stretched out to have a look. The flap had opened in the cupboard and a cigar case shot out, hitting the floor with a slap.

'Now let me see how you get on,' said Ory to herself, her eyes following the cigar case, which slid up and down, occasionally making a little leap.

'I must say you're a brave one,' continued Ory, 'keeping such a firm hold on your innards. To be a cigar case you are indeed – ' suddenly the lid opened and the cigars tumbled all over the floor, where they started a wild dance.

'Ha, ha, ha,' laughed Ory. 'I'm watching a pantomime.'

'A right old mess we have here . . .'

Ory peered round the curtain and saw Halfdan at the door, shaking his head dubiously, while he stared at the floor.

'Yes, how do you like it? This is how us folk live down here.'

'Damn this slithering!' Halfdan who had bent over to pick up the cigars, was thrown over and slapped his hands against the floor.

Ory laughed heartily. 'Isn't it fun?' she said.

'Fun?' repeated Halfdan. He squatted, cigar case in

hand, concentrating every effort on keeping his balance. 'Sleeping is better fun,' he yawned and rubbed his eyes.

'Don't you come here and spoil my mood,' said Ory. Just then a loud crash sounded from the saloon. Halfdan went towards the door to investigate.

'It's the stove! Crikey, the whole thing is in smithereens,' he disappeared and Ory could hear him pick up the pieces. She joined him when she had put on her dark red, woollen dressing-gown.

'Good heavens, what a mess!' she exclaimed. 'The lamp black as a chimney and the floor all wet.' She sat down in a corner of the day-bed.

'The captain mentioned something about a chest,' said Halfdan, when he had gathered all the pieces and got them securely stowed away.

'Yes, it's in the cabin. Have you something to tie it down with?'

'No, but I can use my braces,' said Halfdan and went back to the cabin.

Ory followed and sat down on the chart box.

'That's it then,' said Halfdan, when he had secured the chest. 'Unless madam has some other demand . . .'

'Madam . . .' said Ory and laughed.

'It said in the letter, which was inside the packet you brought from home, that I would have to be on formal terms with you from now on and remember to call you "madam".'

'Pooh,' exclaimed Ory. 'What nonsense.'

'But the captain might be jealous,' said Halfdan with a sly smile.

'Whatever next! Aren't you a bit big for your boots! Had we at least been talking about Hagbart. . . .'

'Well, why didn't you marry him when he asked you to? Then you would have been my sister-in-law.'

'What kind of match would that have been? – A boy still at grammar school and no older than myself!'

'They are all boys before they become men. And he's already a student.'

'But I felt nothing for him,' said Ory, shaking her head.

'That was rather sad,' said Halfdan. 'I think your refusal has made him unhappy for the rest of his days.'

'Oh, he'll get over it – just you wait and see.'

'But can you imagine – he came home and told everybody about it himself – that's how unhappy he was.'

'I have never breathed a word of it to anybody,' Ory put in quickly.

'It must have been embarrassing admitting to something like that,' continued Halfdan. 'Especially to one's own family.'

'Did they tell him off?'

'Well, father did. But mother put in a good word for him. You seem to have quite a bit of that sort of thing on your conscience. Is it true that you've had six suitors?'

'Has it become six now?' Ory blushed and laughed.

'At least now you're married and out of harm's way,' said Halfdan with a sigh. 'But are you happy and contented?'

'Why wouldn't I be?'

'No reason, I just asked.'

'Go and fetch us a couple of glasses of wine, Halfdan. I think we deserve it.'

Halfdan went into the forecabin and returned immediately with a bottle tucked under his arm and two glasses stuck between his fingers.

'Sit down here on the chart box, then you can hold on to the chest and I can hold on to you. Cheers.'

'We'll drink to your new status. Cheers, madam!'

'Cheers, Mr Cabin Boy!' they clinked their glasses and emptied them.

Just then the ship rolled heavily on to her port side and Ory slipped off the box and slid in a squatting position towards the bed, holding her glass raised well above her head.

Halfdan leapt immediately to her side and helped her back.

They drank more wine and chatted. Suddenly Halfdan kissed her cheek.

'What's wrong with you, boy!'

'You aren't mad at me, are you, Ory? I didn't mean to do it, it just happened.'

'Oh, all right then,' said Ory and shook her head. 'But I won't have any more of that sort of thing – just you remember that. What do you think Riber would have said?'

'Why should it worry him? He's kissed enough girls in his time.'

'How do you know?'

'Huh, that much even I know. But he may have told you another story. . . .'

'That's enough of your lip, Halfdan.' Ory felt blood rising to her head and moved away from him.

'It was only meant as a joke,' said Halfdan embarrassed. 'I'm sorry, madam.'

'You can go now,' Ory gave him the glass and got up from the chart box. 'There's nothing more for you to do.'

'You won't tell the captain, will you?' said Halfdan meekly.

'I don't mean you any harm, Halfdan. You may call me madam from now on though. It is after all more appropriate.'

'Well, good night then, madam.'

Then they all knew how Riber had been, thought Ory, when she crawled into bed once more. The officers, the crew Halfdan, everybody. That was why they were so friendly towards her and looked as though they pitied her.

Of course. Just because of that. Oh, dear God, why was she here aboard this ship? What did she want with Riber? Why had she married and left home in the first place? The whole thing was futile and stupid. To be lying here and be shaken to pieces in this revolting bed, that wasn't even her own and which she wouldn't want for her own even if she had it thrown at her.

And it would be an awfully long time before she would

101

see another shore. Sea, ship and seamen would be her sole prospects for weeks and months.

If only she had married Hagbart – how happy she would have been! Tears started pouring down her face as she imagined she longed for Hagbart.

Oh, and this awful weather that went on and on. They had not had a single calm day yet. 'As soon as it has quietened down a bit I'll tell you everything,' answered Riber every time she approached that dreadful issue.

He was obviously only too glad to have the bad weather as a means of delay.

Oh, well, she could wait. She turned on her side, braced her knees against the wall to avoid the worst of the tumult and yawned. She had even grown sleepy and it seemed as though the ship had quietened down. The movement was more akin to being rocked to and fro in a cot.

· 10 ·

The sun was in the meridian. The mate was taking a reading by the sextant, looking through it at the glowing dial. The wind came from astern and the ship, carrying every bit of sail, was making eight knots.

Ory sat on a bench in front of the wheelhouse, her hands resting limply in her lap and a piece of crotcheting between idle fingers. She was wearing a blue striped canvas shirt and had a white, wide-brimmed straw hat on her head. Her face was pale and about her mouth there was an expression of obdurate pain.

She looked at the deep blue ocean with its gentle swells and wished she could lie in the blissful water and be bobbed along on interminable waves, until she were delivered on a shore where everything was the way she had always believed it to be.

The next best thing would be to die. Not to be shipwrecked, but to become sick aboard ship with some slow, consuming illness and waste away quietly and gently.

That is what Riber deserved. Then he would be overcome by contrition such as God required before absolving him of his sins.

Imagine dying on the ocean in weather like this. . . . Riber had said that they would be sailing with the sun for weeks, so if, for example, she was seized by consumption, she would have ample time to die.

She would demand to be carried up on deck every day,

where she would lie on a white bed beneath the sunsail, listening to the soothing rush of wind and the ocean's lamenting song, until one evening death relieved her.

Then she would reach out her pale hand towards Riber and bestow upon him her forgiveness for all the pain he had caused her and tell him she hoped that they would meet before God. She would sigh and turn her dimming eyes towards heaven, seeing her own soul, a single white wing, soaring upward until it vanished in the deep blue.

Her heart swelled and the corners of her mouth quivered. She had to quickly tip her hat forward to hide her face in its shade while she dried her eyes.

Oh, how the torment bore down on her. Her heart was a burden of lead and across her chest lay a weight that prevented her from breathing. Not for a second, day or night, not even during sleep, would the torment cease. Most of the night she lay awake racked with sorrow.

'Mess time, madam,' said Halfdan, who had come aft.

Ory nodded and he walked on.

If only she had not had to attend these meals. She did not have the slightest bit of appetite. But a couple of days ago, when she had appeared neither at dinner, nor at supper, Halfdan had asked what was the matter. When she had answered that nothing was wrong, he had said something must be up, since she was looking so unhappy. The last thing she wanted was for Halfdan or the officers to notice anything and to start gossiping about it.

But it was such a strain. Everything was a strain. Even just to answer a simple greeting from one of the officers made her nervous and gave her clammy hands.

When she entered the mess, Riber was already seated. The officers had lined up by the pantry door, waiting for her to arrive. Halfdan was ladling out tinned meat soup from a blue, patterned tureen at one end of the table.

'Be with you in a moment,' muttered Ory, as she hurried into the saloon, where she left her hat and the crotcheting.

The meal proceeded in gloomy silence. Riber looked

dark and troubled. Ory ate a little of the soup, but could scarcely manage to get down any of the meat. She made a point of passing on the dishes to the officers, which Riber forgot to do. She racked her brain for something to say. This silence must be oppressive for the mates, especially with this extraordinarily beautiful weather and the work aboard ship running smoothly.

'One is hardly aware of being at sea,' she mustered eventually.

'Well, it's exactly like being in a room, all quiet and orderly,' she added a moment later, when the mate, to whom she had addressed herself, looked questioningly at her.

'We aren't always ungallant at sea,' he answered and smiled, throwing a covert glance at Riber.

'Wind and weather doesn't always take those things into account,' said Ory, trying to put on a smile.

'Help yourselves,' Halfdan had put clean plates and a mealy pudding on the table. The pudding was lightly baked on top and spotty with raisins. Ory handed it on to the officers, when Riber had helped himself to a portion.

'Doesn't madam want any?'

'No, it's too doughy.'

'Would you prefer something else?' asked Riber without looking up from his plate. 'Raisins and almonds or pickled fruits? Fetch something, Halfdan.'

'No, thank you. I don't want anything at all,' said Ory.

'It's usual to get an appetite at sea,' said the mate as he tucked into the enormous slab of pudding on the plate in front of him. 'It doesn't seem to be the case with madam.'

'It's the heat,' said Ory and dabbed her face with her handkerchief.

'Some eat more in the heat,' remarked the second mate and blushed with embarrassment at the sound of his own voice.

'I found some flying fish on deck this morning,' said the mate. 'I thought I'd have them fried and give them to madam for supper. Fresh fish might be just the thing.'

'Thank you,' said Ory. 'That would be fun.'

When Riber had finished, he pushed away his plate and rose. The officers hurried and followed suit.

'Thank you,' both of them said and bowed.

'You are welcome,' mumbled Riber.

'Shall I let the sailmaker go ahead with the new sun sail, cap'n?' asked the second mate.

Riber, who was edging his way out from between the table and the long bench that was fixed to the floor, did not answer.

'Or would you rather we let him finish the studding sail, cap'n?'

'The second mate is asking you something,' said Ory who was on her way into the saloon. She stopped and turned towards Riber.

'Hm,' said Riber, putting his hand on her shoulder as he bent his face down towards her better to hear.

Ory ducked away from him with a swooping movement and went into the saloon.

The second mate repeated his question about which job should be done.

'Yes,' said Riber dismissively and made a sweeping gesture with his hand, as he disappeared through the saloon door.

'What the devil is up with the captain these days?' asked the second mate. ' "Yes – he said!" '

'You're telling me . . .' said the mate, thrusting his hands deep down into his trouser pockets.

'Last night on the mid-watch he stood amidships with his arms hanging overboard and his head up in the air. He didn't as much as stir or even make a noise.'

'Maybe he's started taking the position at night,' answered the second mate with a low chuckle. 'This is the fifth day he hasn't touched the sextant.'

'And him, who's usually worried about others not doing it well enough.'

'And the missus is sleeping on the day-bed, when I

come down in the morning,' inserted Halfdan, who was clearing the table.

'Be quiet, boy, they can hear you! Who asked you, anyhow?'

'Surely I'm allowed to speak even if I'm not spoken to.'

'You've got some cheek, boy,' whispered the mate threateningly. 'What else?'

'What'd'ye mean, what else?'

'About them in there,' the mate inclined his goat-like head towards the saloon door.

'I don't go around gossiping,' said Halfdan in a huff and strutted into the pantry with the dishes.

'The missus sleeps on the day-bed, he says. Looks to me like she does a fair bit of running about on deck at night too.'

'Yes,' said the second mate. 'When *he* goes down, *she* comes up.'

'Oh well, enough is enough,' nodded the mate. 'The autocrat has gone to the dogs and there's hardly an ordinary captain left. Do we get our coffee now, boy?' The officers went into their own cabin to fill their pipes.

· 11 ·

Riber, a long, unlit pipe in his hand, sat in the corner of the day-bed in the saloon. He stared ahead with tired eyes and a vacant expression. Occasionally he sighed heavily and changed his position, carefully and unobtrusively, as though he was afraid of making a noise. Beyond the stern windows, whose shutters had been removed, the ocean was a hazy blue; and through the open skylight the sunshine poured in, suffusing the cabin with a golden haze.

'Coffee, captain,' Halfdan entered and put the tray on the table.

'Thank you, my boy,' Riber pulled himself together and lit his pipe. 'Tell madam that the coffee is ready.'

Halfdan went to the sleeping quarters, peered in through the curtain at the entrance and announced to Ory, who was washing her hands, that he had brought the coffee.

Ory came into the saloon and sat down on the bench on the sloping stern.

'Coffee's getting cold,' said Riber after a while.

'I don't want any,' mumbled Ory.

Riber slurped his coffee and puffed, every so often, on his pipe. He retreated further into the corner of the day-bed.

It was quiet and hot. Not a sound was heard from deck. Now and then the water lapped softly against the stern.

Ory leaned back and shut her eyes.

Today it was a fortnight since Riber's confession. Fourteen days, which had seemed like as many weeks spent in the throes of agony. She had been prepared for a lot, but the foulness of what she had learnt seemed to her beyond human imagination. What she could not understand was how she had had the presence of mind to listen to it all, to put her questions calmly, while her blood ran hot and cold and she felt herself fall from abyss to abyss. Not until she had gone over everything time and again, ascertained and reascertained all and Riber had restated the facts, answered her every question and assured her that there was no more, had she uttered the chilling cry that had made him leap from the day-bed and stand as if numbed in the middle of the floor.

It might not have seemed so terrible if only Riber had been less hardened. But he simply could not begin to understand why she was so upset. That at least was what he made out and it seemed as if he believed it, or he would surely have withheld some of the stories or attempted to screen them. How degenerate he must be – and how devoid of religion! But he called himself a Christian and actually believed he was. What confused concepts he must be harbouring. She herself had unfortunately worried far too little about these matters, but there was at least the notion in her that she must be conscious of sin, while Riber – he was a heathen, yes, nothing less than a heathen.

From now on she would take her relationship with God far more seriously. This issue would lead her to salvation. It had already begun. She had started to pray every morning and every night and to read a little bit each day from her book of devotional stories or the Bible itself. If only she could acquire the proper spirit of love. Love was all, the kind of love that would suffer everything, forgive everything and kindle hope from the ashes. It was this kind of love she did not possess; her soul was not meek. Far from it. And the commandment: 'Judge not', seemed to her the most difficult one of all. She *did* judge Riber, she simply could not help it, she judged him as one whose whole life was an uninterrupted chain of utter depravity and sin.

And in that the Bible supported her. It did preach judgment, punishment and perdition for profligates and the Church catechism held that fornication and lechery were the most terrible of sins, or at least the most shocking. Then it was not she who judged him, but God's Word. And, strictly speaking, it was not him she judged, but his actions.

According to Riber she ought not to concern herself with any of it. She ought not to delve into his past, but to look forward to the new life he would live with and for her alone. She ought to do this and she ought to do that. It was easy to talk; there must have been things he 'ought to' have done, but this business of 'ought to' was something he had not bothered about then. And now he imagined that he could come to her with the demand that everything that embarrassed him now, but had previously been his life and joy, should be dead and buried and out of the world. If he could demand, or think like that, it showed that he had no idea of what had taken place and could not see that she was like someone stuck in a quagmire and fated to stay there till she drew her last breath. What good did it do, even if she told herself a hundred times to think about other things – there *was* nothing else. These filthy scenes came to her continually. When the officers or any of the crew walked past her, she asked herself: 'I wonder if he's been like Riber. . . .' And about all the men she had known in her whole life, she asked the same question. All her imagination centered on this one thing and she could feel an agonized, voluptuous shudder by conjuring up Riber in those situations. This made her want to hear him talk more about it, have him tell her all the stories over and over again, with every particular and always with more detail. He didn't like it: 'Be merciful,' he pleaded. He suffered too much from it.

But what about her? Besides – what he called suffering. . . . The whole thing seemed to mean nothing to him. She had noticed that if she didn't draw any attention to it for even half a day, his spirits would rise immediately.

What an incredible silence! It was like being on a ghost-ship. She dozed off.

A light thud made her open her eyes and straighten up. Riber was sleeping on the day-bed, with his elbow on the arm rest and his head supported in his hand. From between his knees protruded the mouth-piece of the long pipe which must have slipped onto the floor.

Ory watched him. His lips were shut tight and the corners of his mouth were peculiarly drawn beneath his blond moustache. Between his eyebrows were three furrows, the middle one longer and more pronounced than the other two. His eyebrows were knitted and the lids beneath them were red and swollen. His broad forehead was creased and his skull glistened above it. He drew his breath lightly and without a sound.

It seemed to Ory she was seeing him for the first time. He had changed so much. It was like seeing a stranger. His face had become so old and gaunt.

What a different expression his face must have had when he had slept with those he had paid to sleep with. Ory rose and walked stealthily towards the day-bed. A look of disgust hovered about her half-opened lips and supporting her hands on the table, she imagined how he had looked that time – or that time – or that time. . . .

Riber suddenly gave a deep sigh, his eyelids lifted and Ory, who had dashed back, shuddered at the eerie, strangely glazed look that for a moment rested on her, before the twitching lids shut again.

A moment later he shouted out in a forced, somnolent voice: 'Hold on, Emmy!' Whereupon he passed his hand over his eyes, sat upright and was awake.

'Why did you shout?' asked Ory, who had once again pulled back in fright.

'Did I shout?'

'Yes, you shouted: "Hold on, Emmy!"'

'That wasn't me,' said Riber and lit his pipe.

Ory looked indignant. 'How can you say a thing like that, when I stood right here and heard it!'

'Well, I can't remember shouting.'

'You are dreaming then?'

'One has to sleep to dream and I have not slept.'

'Didn't you! You slept soundly enough for your pipe to fall on the floor. And I've been standing here for a long time, looking at you without you noticing.'

'Have you been looking at me, Aurora?' Riber reached out his hand somewhat timidly towards her.

'Still you persist in telling me you haven't slept!?'

'I feel as though I've just been sitting here, thinking,' said Riber, letting his hand fall. 'I am not accustomed to sleeping any more either by day or night.'

'Why is that? You who have such a clear conscience!'

'My conscience is no worse than others,' answered Riber feebly. 'And has no reason to be.'

'Why do you always have to bring those "others" into it? What have the others got to do with you? If you were a Christian, which you insist you are, then you would know how your conscience ought to be.'

'I read the Bible last night,' said Riber quietly, 'and according to what I read there, people were no better at that time – rather the opposite.'

'There you go again with your "people". Of course there were many immoral people about at the time of the Old Testament, but if you had read the New Testament you would have seen what Jesus demands.'

'I did do that as well. And I read there that Jesus said to the woman who was caught in adultery: "Neither do I condemn thee." That I thought was a beautiful thing to say.'

To Ory's ears his words sounded like blasphemy. And in addition she felt a vehement resentment for the fact that he had found something to cover himself with.

'And you dare to apply that to yourself?' she asked,

folding her arms across her chest.

'Why not? Anyone may derive consolation from the scriptures.'

'The repentant, yes, but not the haughty and the hardened.'

'I'm neither one, nor the other, Aurora. I'm simply a human being who is not as black as you make him out to be.'

'You've made yourself black, not I. Black! You are worse than black, you are obscene!'

'I have heard that so often lately,' said Riber and smiled glumly.

'Besides, you are forgetting half of the text,' continued Ory triumphantly: "Go and sin no more."'

'I do not sin any more.'

'Of course not, here aboard ship you haven't got a chance. But where did you get to that Sunday night in London, when you ran off and left me with Mrs Suder?'

Riber gave a start and his eyes opened wide.

'And where had you been that evening in Gravesend, when you came aboard in the middle of the night?'

'Well, I'm blowed! When it comes to it, women are the lowest forms of creation,' said Riber, shattered by this remark and shaking his head indignantly. 'Aren't you ashamed of yourself?' he looked severely at Ory.

'Aren't you,' said Ory, 'who has taught me to think this way? Who was it that told me Captain Smith had gone with a woman when his wife was waiting for him aboard ship? Who recounted it as a casual everyday occurrence. . . . Your only objection being that she wasn't appetising enough.'

'For shame,' said Riber and spat.

'Yes, for shame! Do you think I would have invented this by myself? My whole misfortune is that everything has been sullied. From now on I'll imagine disgusting and horrible things about absolutely everybody.'

Riber's pipe had gone out long ago and he put it down on the sofa and rose. He grabbed his pointed, white felt hat and walked towards the door.

Ory ran after him. 'Tell me about your dream . . . please, you *must* tell me,' she tugged at his arm.

'What kind of a trap is this?' he looked apprehensive and at a loss.

'When you sat there on the day-bed and called out: "Emmy".'

'I didn't know I called for anybody with the name "Emmy".'

'That is only because you daren't tell me.'

He turned abruptly and wanted to go, but Ory held him tightly.

'Please, be good enough to tell me,' she begged. 'Just so that I won't have *that* as well to worry about. . . . Come and sit down,' she grabbed both his hands and tried to pull him along.

'You really confuse me, Aurora,' he let himself reluctantly be pulled along to the day-bed, where she made him sit down.

'What is it you want me to tell you?'

'Well, listen,' said Ory, as she sat down beside him and turned towards him. 'You were sleeping here on the sofa, because you *were* sleeping, whether you remember it or not and then, all of a sudden, you shouted: "Hold on, Emmy!" '

Riber shook his head.

'Think about it. I can wait. Try to remember how it was.'

Riber pondered for a while.

'Aha,' he said and snapped his fingers. 'Wait – I think it's coming. Of course I was dreaming! Now I've got it! I was standing on the forecastle in a full gale, when an upturned boat appeared up ahead on the leeward side. I saw heads and arms of people clinging on and you were among them, but you looked like you were going to let go. I pulled off my reefer so that I could jump out and I shouted with all my might: "Hold on, Aurora!" '

'No, Emmy.'

'Then I must have mistaken the name, for it was you I saw in my dream.'

'But who is "Emmy"?'

'How the hell should I know? I know nobody of that name.'

'But you *must*, how else would it come to your subconscious mind? . . . .'

'Emmy, Emmy,' Riber toyed with the name.

'Can't you think of anybody you know with that name – when you really try hard?'

'No,' said Riber unsteadily.

'Oh, yes, you can! I can see it in your eyes! Tell me . . .' she moved up closer and put her hand on his.

'No, Aurora, let me be! If I had ever known anybody with that name, what difference would it make?'

'None at all – of course not.' Ory, her blood racing at fever pitch, when she realized she had guessed right, assumed a casual expression. 'Just so – then you might as well tell me, Riber.'

'Yes,' said Riber, with downcast eyes. 'It was her I was with that time in London.'

'Before you went home and got married,' said Ory, finishing his sentence for him.

'Before I went home and got married,' repeated Riber, as though he fumbled for the words. He felt despondent. Why did he not keep quiet or refuse. . . . Previously it had been because he had wanted to confess everything and get an absolution. He had imagined he could turn over a new leaf afterwards and that it would make his marriage into that which he had always wanted. But now, when he knew how she reacted! It was sheer madness! Yet every time she asked, in a friendly and open manner, as she had done just now, he *would* blurt out the truth.

'And her name was Emmy?' asked Ory.

'Yes, it was. She was a beautiful young lady, and what's more a vicar's daughter from Yorkshire. It was my married cousin, old Ole Riber, who introduced me to her. We'd been to a ball at the dance hall – where you and I

went, you remember – and she was standing at the
entrance without a partner. I didn't want to go with her
because I was thinking of you, but Ole pulled my leg and
asked if I didn't have what it takes. He was going off with
another woman. She took my arm and invited me to
accompany her home and in the cab she told me her name
was Emmy Wood.'

'Was she so beautiful?' asked Ory with curiosity.

'Marvellous,' said Riber and seemed for a moment lost
in thought. 'As fine and as proper as a lady. And she had
a nice flat in a respectable neighbourhood. Drawing-
room, dining-room and a large bedroom with lace
curtains draped round the bed.'

'What did you do when you got there?'

'She gave me wine and cigars and sat down at the piano
to sing and play.'

'Was she any good?'

'Excellent. I probably sat for an hour listening to her.'

'What then?'

'Stop it now, Aurora.'

'Did you stay all night?'

'Yes, it was bright daylight when I woke up.'

'Did you kiss her before you got up?'

'I can't remember.'

'Doesn't one usually?'

'That depends. . . .'

'Was it embarrassing to say "goodbye"?'

'No,' said Riber sincerely. 'I asked her how much she
wanted and she answered: 'I never set terms, Sir.''

'What did you do then?'

'I left eighteen shillings on her dressing table.'

'Do you think that was enough?'

'By my own estimate it was enough.'

'And the day after you went home and got married,'
said Ory, after a pause, in a cutting voice. She rose and
started to pace up and down on the floor. Her face
twitched as though in a cramp.

'Here we go!' exclaimed Riber. 'Why in heaven's name

can you never stop raking over these things?'

'Because it is so ghastly.' Ory stopped, turned about and looked at him. 'Oh, you don't know how it is,' she ran towards him and fell down at his feet. 'I am so full of fear and pain that I prostrate myself before you who have caused it and beg you to comfort and help me.'

'Then what can I do for you? . . .' he took her head between his hands.

'You shouldn't have married, Riber, not me at any rate. Can't you understand what it is like not to have had the faintest idea . . .' she sought to hide her face. 'And why did you want to get married when you were enjoying life, as you were? Or why didn't you at least marry someone like Emmy?'

'Because I longed for something better, Aurora.'

'Something better,' she threw back her head and looked at him with flashing eyes. 'And do you imagine you can come into something better just like that? Oh no, you ought to have chosen someone more suitable. I for one can't put up with a man like you. Just imagine if it had all been different, if I had been your first and only one – don't you wish that, Riber?' she looked at him with shining eyes.

'I don't wish for the impossible, Aurora,' said Riber and sighed.

Ory looked astounded at him.

'Would you rather see me put on an act for you?' asked Riber and stroked her hair.

'Let me be – you are the most loathsome human being in the world!' shouted Ory and jumped up violently. 'I hate you! I detest you! I wish I had fallen dead when you first set eyes on me. There can't be a woman anywhere foul enough to be fit for you.'

Riber turned white about his nostrils.

'You are a traitor,' he said, accentuating each word. 'Judas Escariot, who sold Jesus for thirty pieces of silver, was an angel compared with you. What harm have I done to you?'

'Poor you,' answered Ory. 'I may well be as wretched as is humanly possible, but I wouldn't change my position with you for anything on earth!'

'Go to hell!' said Riber furiously. 'Won't you let me be what I am. . . . Do I bother you nowadays? Do I ask anything of you? Have I ever once forced myself on you since this occurred? So, won't you leave me in peace, you bloody tart!' He thumped the table with such force that Ory jumped. Without a word she rose and went into the cabin, where she sat down on the chart box and started to weep.

'Bloody tart . . .' he had dared to call *her* that. He! If he had possessed the merest flicker of conscience, he would have been so ashamed and mortified that he would have lain down to be trodden on. She should have been the one to have had something like that to confess! It wasn't the first time it had ended with him swearing and banging his fist down on the table. Oh dear, oh dear, what could she do. How long could she endure this agony?

And then his incredible stubbornness – it filled her with a rage that made her blood boil. He would always hold back when she wanted to show him how appallingly he had conducted himself. He flaunted outright what he considered his dues. Admit to one's wife, that on the way to the wedding – no, there were no words for such beastliness. And even to say how beautiful, fine and proper the women had been. . . . Good God! What difference was there then between herself and all the others? And now he had persuaded himself that he loved her. Oh, how could he utter a word like that with his filthy mouth!

If only she had been ashore! She could have fled through the streets of London, slept during the night in a shed somewhere and run along again at the crack of dawn. On and on, until she collapsed from fatigue and was found by a nice, old man, who would take her home to his wife and let her stay there, hidden from the world. But to be here as a prisoner on this ship with only the ocean all around. . . . With no possible escape unless she jumped into the water. She had thought of that more than once. It often seemed like the only solution.

If only she could summon up the courage to do it. This evening, for instance, when there was only one man at the helm and everything had gone quiet. Just sit on the hammock netting at the stern, give a push and fall backward into the water. The sound would be lost in all the other splashing behind there. Nobody would notice. The whole night might pass and the morning dawn, before she would be missed. Then Riber would creep around stealthily, searching high and low for her, until at last he braced himself to ask first Halfdan and the officers, then the whole crew, if they had seen 'madam'. There would be a great commotion and panic in the whole ship, but at first they would all just stand there as if paralysed and no one would dare to say aloud what he was thinking. Riber would go below, lock himself into his cabin and behave like a lunatic. Or he would jump overboard to join her in death. How it would gnaw at him and torment him that he had called her a 'bloody tart' and not received a word of forgiveness before she left him for ever. She would make sure he did not. When he came and clamoured for forgiveness as usual, she would not deign to give him an answer, but stare right past him with a rigid gaze, or just go on weeping.

She had cried buckets already during the whole fortnight. How could a human being possibly produce so many tears. She put down her soaking wet handkerchief, took another one out of the chest of drawers and went on crying.

Hours passed by, dusk fell and Ory remained sitting on the chart box. Her legs were stiff and tired, but she didn't move.

Why hadn't Riber come and apologized. . . . What was he doing in there? Maybe he had fallen asleep again.

Just then she could hear Riber get up and start to shuffle about. What kind of noise was that? A cracking of limbs and groaning . . . Was that him crying?

She sneaked towards the curtain and peered through. Riber was standing in the middle of the floor doing gymnastics. In his hands he held the two weights which were tied to the ends of a rope hanging around his neck.

So he was capable of that, the monster! 'But just you wait and I'll give you something else to think about.' She had no doubt that she would jump overboard tonight.

When it was teatime, Ory excused herself with a headache. It would be impossible to sit at table with all the others and to show her tear-stained face.

She remained below a good while after it had gone eight bells. Then she went up. Riber had not approached her all evening.

She leaned on the stern railing with her elbows and rested her head in her hands. Phosphorescent lights played and twinkled on the broken ridges of the small, dark waves in their wake.

If they were to notice when she jumped and threw a lifebelt to her, would she manage to get a hold of it? The impression it would make on Riber would be the same, even if she was pulled up again. If only she could be sure of being rescued. It was, after all, a big sacrifice to die, especially as a suicide, because she would be condemned to hell.

'Aurora,' a voice whispered and at the same time a hand was laid on her shoulder.

She moved a little without looking up.

'I really am sorry, Aurora.'

'Don't bother to apologize. Tomorrow you'll call me a "bloody tart" once again.'

'No, Aurora, I won't ever do that again. What do I gain by doing it? I am the one who suffers most from it.'

'You!'

'Yes, Aurora. I suffer so much that I often worry about my sanity. I am not accustomed to adversity – I can't cope with it.'

'Oh, I think you are coping wonderfully. While I was

crying my eyes out in the cabin and thinking I would go to pieces, you were quite contentedly doing exercises in the saloon.'

'Contentedly,' there was an edge of pain in Riber's voice. 'I try anything to chase away for a while the thoughts that haunt me. When I sit brooding like that my head gets so confused. I hear voices speaking to me, strange contemptuous voices and I see two of everything.'

'What do you see two of?'

'Everything. A couple of times I've also seen something else, something terrible. Have you ever seen anything like that?'

'How would I know? You haven't told me what it is.'

'It's something dark, wet and slimy that may appear suddenly in broad daylight. The texture reminds me of a wet fur seal, but the shape is neither animal nor man. The legs are no more than a foot high and the feet are round lumps. The body is as wide as a stuffed sack and the head droops, with dead, narrow eyes and a large, jutting chin. I don't see a mouth, but a long, sad nose.'

'Aren't you frightened?' asked Ory, perturbed.

'I'm not really frightened, but I feel strangely feeble. I would have liked to tell you when it's there once, just to see if it looks the same to you or if you could see it at all, but I can neither speak nor move.'

'What happens to it afterwards?'

'That I don't know. It's there only for short spells. And, funnily enough, it reminds me of something and I worry myself sick to know what it is.'

'I think it is God's punishment. He wants you to repent.'

'I think it is more that I'm drinking too much.'

'Do you drink at night?'

'Yes, to enable me to sleep. I drink and read the Bible. Last night I emptied a whole bottle of brandy – to no effect. I didn't get drunk – not in the least.'

'Are you going to take up drinking as well now?'

'What can I do? I am haunted by fear. Fear of your

next interrogation. Just thinking about it is like a cold wind in an open wound.'

'It's your own fault. Had I noticed that you were more repentant it would make it easier for me to forgive and forget.'

'Forgive,' said Riber gently. 'Do you think it is only me who needs forgiveness?'

'What do you mean by that?' asked Ory sharply.

'I mean the day of reckoning will come and you will have to answer to yourself and God for how you have treated me.'

'That you should talk about the reckoning! You certainly have enough on your conscience to be talking about when the time comes.'

'I have laid my sins bare.'

'Bare, indeed!' said Ory contemptuously.

'Haven't I been open?'

'Not at all. You never meant to tell me about the time you fell ill.'

'Oh, Aurora, Aurora, won't you let me be,' Riber went on his knees and grabbed her dress imploringly.

'Was she also a beautiful young lady?'

Riber rose and watched Ory with despair. Then he tilted his head back and looked up at the sparkling starry night.

'Won't you tell me,' pleaded Ory. 'Just this once.'

'I have never known that a child could be such a heartless executioner,' said Riber, shaking his head quietly. 'Yes, you are a child and that is your only excuse.' He turned round and left her.

Ory watched him go. He walked forward to the forecastle and remained sitting there for many hours.

· 12 ·

The *Orion* had been becalmed for eleven days in the still waters of the Bay of Florida. The air was suffocating and the sun so hot that the pitch had melted in the seams between the deck planks. The crew members had gone a deep brown, they walked with their bare feet on the burning hot deck and although they wore only cotton shirts and canvas trousers, they were soaked in sweat.

Every evening at sunset there were flashes of lightning without thunder. They were so fiery and flashed so rapidly that it seemed as though the whole horizon was ablaze. During the days the ocean was as smooth as a mirror and blinding white, but then it would suddenly start to roll in heavy swells that broke against the ship with leaden weight, making her pitch and toss like a monster writhing in cramp. But it lasted no more than about ten minutes, then the ocean went back to rest.

The conditions aboard were on the whole unpleasant. The crew suffered from the heat and the long calm dulled them. The drinking water had started to turn brackish and everybody, men and officers alike, had diarrhoea.

Riber, who had been deaf and blind to everything, even while they had followed the trade wind, was now roaming about everywhere at all hours. He scolded and gave orders, finding nothing done according to his wishes.

He often had rows with the first mate, whose stubbornness and provocative way of answering irritated him almost beyond his endurance.

The relationship between Riber and Ory had, if anything, got worse. She could no longer make him answer a question or tell her any more stories. Every time she asked him, he shuddered and his face started to twitch like a madman's and then he would run away. Below, in the captain's cabin, the stern windows were left open night and day, and the skylight was removed, but still there was never a breath of air passing through.

'The Son of man goeth as it is written of him: but woe unto that man by whom the son of man is betrayed. It had been good for that man if he had not been born. . . .' Riber was doing his nightly reading in the saloon, by the light of the lamp hanging from the skylight. He wore only a shirt, his legs and feet were bare. On the table in front of him lay the open Bible and on the floor up against the day-bed, stood a half emptied bottle of brandy and a beer glass.

'. . . but woe unto that man who is betrayed . . .' muttered Riber, leaning back in the day-bed. 'No . . . woe unto that man by whom the son of man is betrayed . . ,' he corrected himself. His mind was wandering, lost in thought he stared ahead of him with unseeing eyes.

A sigh brought him back from his reveries. He looked towards the sloping stern where Ory lay on the leather cushions by the open windows, between two sheets and with a pillow under her head. She had just turned over in her sleep.

'. . . woe unto her who betrays,' said Riber faintly and shook his fist towards Ory.

Six bells sounded from the deck. The sound startled Riber and he leapt up and was in the middle of the floor in one jump. He raised his hand to his ear, ducked his head and listened.

Strike the bell,
the time to quell,
to stop the time no man befell . . .

he whispered and sat down again. He grabbed for the bottle of brandy and the glass, poured himself a drink and gulped it down.

'Damn it!' He had never had a crossing like this before. It seemed as though the wind had died. Becalmed here in this poisonous heat, moving knot by laborious knot for weeks through an ocean still as a winding sheet! He grabbed his hair by his temples and snarled through clenched teeth and dirty lips.

All things were against him. Men, animals, the growth of the soil – nonsense – God, men, wind and weather.

Woe unto him who betrays! Woe unto the lot of them. They were all laughing behind his back – the mate, the crew – yes – even the rascal of a cabin boy. What rabble! Because they had realized that he was a broken man they thought they could lead him by the nose. The mate with his: 'But my good captain. . . .' He ought to belt him one across the face.

Christ Almighty! He would show them that he was nobody's 'good captain'. He would teach them to out-Herod Herod . . . he would . . . he would . . . he would – throw them all overboard . . ! When they arrived at Pensacola he would at any rate, turn his back on all of them and go off to the Indians.

If only the wind would blow! 'God, you Almighty Sinner, why won't you give us some wind! You and your big talk about betrayal!' he bent over the Bible and read: 'The Lord Jesus, on the night when he was betrayed . . .' then he pushed away the book, looked up through the skylight and muttered: 'Carl Adolph Riber took the bread on the night when he was betrayed, gave his thanks, broke it and said: "Take, eat, this is my body."'

Yes, he had tasted the bitter bread Aurora had offered him and eaten thereof, eaten unto his own death and damnation.

Here it was again – this giddiness. He trembled in every joint and large beads of sweat appeared on his forehead. His hands lay feebly on the table and his mouth was half open. Something was forcing his eyes to squint sideways and he could feel his hair stand on end.

There – to the left, under the bench at the stern, rigid, lifeless, still, wet and with the drooping head.

Riber was erect as a pillar. Beads of sweat rolled off his nose and dripped onto the open pages of the Bible. His eyes remained transfixed on the creature.

'Slomen,' he whispered suddenly with a deep breath. 'Yes, Slomen,' he repeated. 'Why haven't I known your name before. . . . What do you want with me, Slomen?'

'No, no, please, don't go before you've answered me. You and I are one.' But Slomen had gone and Riber's head sank down on the table.

A numbness crept through his limbs. His whole body felt dead. But in his temples was a slow beating and threadlike, ice-cold ripples ran through the back of his head.

Ory moved about restlessly on her berth. She threw off the top sheet and sat upright, exhaling heavily, as if to blow away the heat.

Poor Riber, he had fallen asleep across the Bible. Oh, if only she had not been married to him – then she could have gone over there and comforted and taken care of him. He really was in need of care these days, gaunt and ghastly as he was and with such foul breath. But she didn't dare to approach him in case he misunderstood and made a grab for her.

She could love him as another human being, he was after all a decent, nice and clever man in many ways. But to be his wife and to be 'one flesh' with him – good gracious, no!

But looking at him as a close acquaintance or even a girlfriend. . . . Yes, that was it – a girlfriend – since he had told her so many confidences. . . . As soon as they were back home she could live with her parents again. Or if Riber preferred, by herself. She obviously had to go on calling herself Mrs Riber for the rest of her life. . . . But he could go back to living the way he had done before. As long as she was rid of him, that would not bother her in the least.

But there were still a couple of things she would like to get out of him. That time in the Klingenberg gardens – in the open – just like the animals. . . .

And also how he had felt after his first visit to one of those houses when he was only fourteen. . . .

Riber had raised his head and read once again from the Bible: 'And whosoever shall offend one of these little ones that believe in me, it were better for him that a millstone were hanged about his neck, and he were cast into the sea.'

'. . . offend one of these little ones . . .' – what was meant by that?

It could not be children, they did not have the sense to become offended.

'You should go to bed and get some sleep, Riber.'

Riber looked up from the book and his eyes roamed all around the saloon.

'You ought to lie down, Riber,' repeated Ory.

'Yes, lie down. . . . Lie down in perpetual rest.' Riber looked at Ory with eyes that glinted metallically. 'Bid me goodnight, Aurora.'

'Goodnight? Why, it is morning!'

'Is it morning? Morning is like spring. Life begins again. Call me Adolph, Aurora.'

'All the others have called you Adolph, so why should I?'

'No, that's right. Call me Slomen. Have you seen Slomen?'

'Slomen!' said Ory. 'What nonsense is this now?'

'Slomen was here again last night. He smiled at me.'

'One wouldn't think you were in your right mind the way you talk.'

'Oh yes,' said Riber, 'at last I'm in my right mind, now I understand everything. I have offended one of the little ones and that is you, Aurora.'

'Me? What does that matter . . . but it just goes to show!'

'I don't ask you ever again to call me Adolph. No, never. Between us there is only hostility.'

'No, not hostility. We can still be friends, Riber.'

'Oh yes, friends, friends, friends. . . . If you believe that you are my friend – then Heaven help me! Not a friend, not a wife, not anything else either. I'm scared of you, purely and simply scared. As soon as we reach shore I'll go off to the Indians.'

'Good morning.' Halfdan entered with a brush and a dust-pan.

'You should put out the lamp, Riber,' said Ory, 'it's bright day-light.'

Riber rose, turned down the wick and blew out the flame.

'What the devil! I think there's a wind and nobody is doing anything.' Riber ran out. His bare feet thudded against the waxed floor surface.

'Does madam want coffee?' asked Halfdan.

'Yes, please, I'll have some coffee.' Halfdan left and Ory crawled down from the ledge in her long nightgown and stubbed her foot on one of Riber's weights which were lying on the bench. Then she went into the sleeping quarters and started washing.

'Coffee's ready,' called Halfdan shortly afterwards.

'Put it on the table. What was that noise on deck?'

'It was the captain who hit the mate.'

'Wait a moment, Halfdan.' Ory put on her dressing-gown and went into the saloon. 'Did he hit him?'

'I'll say he did!'

'But why?'

'I was on my way from the galley with the coffee when I saw the captain talking with the mate and all of a sudden the mate lay flat out on the deck with the captain on top.'

'What did the mate do?'

'Nothing. He just lay there and didn't as much as bat

an eyelid. The captain spat in his face and the mate just said: "Be my guest". But here he comes. . . .'

Halfdan left the cabin and seconds later Riber entered. His shirt was torn across the chest, his breathing rapid and his hands, which he held out in front of him, were trembling.

'I've given the mate a licking,' he said, out of breath.

'And I suppose you consider it an act of heroism?' asked Ory and looked at him contemptuously.

'The weather is just as before – not a breath of wind. I'm sick and tired, Aurora.'

'Why don't you try going to bed at night?'

'Bed? What am I supposed to do there?'

'Go and lie down now – you look terrible.'

'Yes, Aurora.' He held onto the table and fumbled along the wall.

Ory watched his powerful legs underneath the short shirt.

'What about that time in the Klingenberg gardens with the waitress . . . ?' She didn't get to finish. A roar, like that of a sick animal, stopped her and at the same time Riber ducked as if to avoid a blow. He turned his head slowly and looked at Ory who sat on the day-bed drinking coffee.

'Well, goodness! Just telling me that is the least you could do.'

Riber threw back his head and jerked it from side to side. Then he walked across to the bench and picked up the weights which lay there. He wrapped the rope they were attached to twice around his neck.

'I can't see that your gymnastics are doing you any good.'

'The Lord Jesus on the night when he was betrayed,' muttered Riber. He jumped on the bench, then onto the ledge and disappeared through the window.

Ory heard a splash and the sound of water rushing to engulf his heavy body.

PANDORA PRESS

Pandora Press is a feminist press, an imprint of Routledge & Kegan Paul. Our list is varied – we publish new fiction, reprint fiction, history, biography and autobiography, social issues, humour – written by women and celebrating the lives and achievements of women the world over. For further information about Pandora Press books, please write to the Mailing List Dept. at Pandora Press, 11 New Fetter Lane, London EC4P 4EE or in the USA at 35 West 35th Street, New York, NY 10001–2291. Some Pandora titles you will enjoy ▶

ORANGES ARE NOT THE ONLY FRUIT

Jeanette Winterson

'Like most people I lived for a long time with my mother and father. My father liked to watch the wrestling, my mother liked to wrestle. . .'

'The achievement of this novel is to make us squirm with laughter, then make us acknowledge how utterly sad it is when the needs of self-preservation turn what has been sacred into a joke.'

Roz Kaveney, *Times Literary Supplement*

'*Oranges* is a brilliant first novel – at once witty, gripping, imaginative and touching.'

Time Out

Paper £4.50   Fiction 086358 042 4
Winner of the 1985 Publishing for People Prize
for First Novel

THIS PLACE

Andrea Freud Loewenstein

'An energetic and passionate novel which grips the reader's attention with unholy force. It is an extraordinary evocation of a closed world – female bodies and female minds struggling against an imprisonment equally dire whether enforced or self-imposed, and written with charity and understanding.'

Fay Weldon

'Loewenstein vividly creates, through a naturalistic fidelity to voice and description, a stifling inferno.'

Michele Roberts

Cloth £9.95   Fiction 086358 039 4
Paper £4.95   086358 040 8

CHARLEYHORSE

Cecil Dawkins

This is an explosive gallop through the family fortunes of mother and daughter on their huge ranch in Kansas.

Mother is a megalomaniac, daughter as stubborn as the bulls she manages; Cecil Dawkins' novel reworks traditional Western themes and is guaranteed to make you laugh, cry and see red.

Cecil Dawkins lives in New Mexico.

Cloth £9.95   Fiction 086358 096 3
Pandora edition not available in USA or Canada

NATURAL SELECTION

Margaret Mulvihill

Maureen works as a slave in a London publishing house and lives on the borders of literary London. Life is a series of groggy mornings, tedious days working on other people's manuscripts and planning illicit meetings with Martin. Until a certain manuscript falls mysteriously into her hands. . .

This witty novel describes a publishing world filled with sex, adultery, plagiarism, opportunism . . . as well as books.

To be read in the bath while eating expensive chocolates.

Cloth £9.95   Fiction 086358 064 5
Paper £3.95   086358 058 0

A WOMAN CALLED EN

Tomie Ōhara

Written by a major modern Japanese novelist, this book won two major literary awards on its publication in Japan.

Based on fact, the novel is set in seventeenth century Japan and centres round En who at four years old is confined with her family to a single house, isolated from society and human contact, when her father falls from political favour. There she remains for forty years but she prevails, strong and refusing to be defeated.

Written in the formal classical style of the seventeenth century, this novel is nevertheless a modern novel, movingly written and painfully felt.

Cloth £9.95   Fiction 086358 079 3
Paper £3.95   086358 082 3

LITTLE TOURS OF HELL

Tall Tales of Food and Holidays

Josephine Saxton

Painting holidays, pregnant holidays, ghastly weekends and reckless rendezvous . . . these are just a few Saxton scenarios to help you get away from it all, with these cautionary tales about campers, hampers and oily foreign muck for gastronomiques and holiday makers everywhere.

These stories are specifically concerned with the more macabre or stultifying aspects of eating and holidaying. Josephine Saxton is able to unravel the disturbing implications behind the most innocent and everyday activities with an acute and very witty eye for detail in sharp and brilliant prose.

Cloth £9.95   Fiction 086358 094 7   176pp
Paper £3.95   086358 095 5

STEPPING OUT

Edited by Ann Oosthuizen

This imaginative collection of short stories
celebrates friendship between women and
explores the new lives that women are leading
today. The stories range from love stories to
friendships and betrayals, to the relationship
between sisters and women in conflict with
contributions from
Anna Livia
Honora Bartlett
Barbara Burford
Michelene Wandor
Ann Oosthuizen
Marsha Rowe
Jackie Kay
Moy McCrory
Andrea Loewenstein
Jo Jones
Sara Maitland

Paper £4.95   Fiction 086358 488 3   176pp

PASSION FRUIT

Romantic Fiction with a Twist

Edited by Jeanette Winterson

A collection of short romances which adds a
new and startling dimension to the traditional
scenario of love, lust and marriage with stories
from:
Rebecca Brown
Angela Carter
Laurie Colwin
Fiona Cooper
Sara Maitland
Bobby Ann Mason
Marge Piercy
Josephine Saxton
Aileen La Tourette
Lorna Tracey
Michelene Wandor
Fay Weldon

Paper £3.95   Fiction 086358 070 X   200pp

AUTOBIOGRAPHY OF A CHINESE GIRL

Hsieh Ping-Ying

With an introduction by Elisabeth Croll

This is the story of Hsieh Ping-Ying, a Chinese girl born at the beginning of this century who rejected the traditions of the old order and eventually became one of China's leading women writers.

At school, she unwrapped the binding on her feet so that she could run freely with the other children. As a young woman she went into the army in order to escape an arranged marriage. As an adult she was charged with being a communist and imprisoned.

Hsieh Ping-Ying's story takes us back to the heart of pre-revolutionary China. She describes her relationship with her family: with her mother and with her grandmother and the difficulties she faced rejecting traditional constraints in order to live as an independent woman.

Paper £4.95   Autobiography 086358 052 1
244p

DARING TO DREAM

Utopian stories by United States women:
1836–1919

Carol Farley Kessler

Carol Farley Kessler has unearthed an
extraordinary assortment of visionary writing,
writings which encapsulate all the yearnings of a
vanished generation for a future which has still
to be made. Some women write with irony,
describing journeys through time and space to
parallel but inverted worlds where sober-suited
women run commerce and affairs of state while
men either prink and preen in beribboned
breeches, or are weakened by the burden of
unending housework. Other writers lay out
complicated blueprints for a non-sexist society.
One woman dreams, touchingly, of a fantastic
future where men get up in the night to comfort
crying children. The stories demonstrate that
even in the early nineteenth century women
were arguing that male and female 'character
traits' were the product of their roles, not of
their biology; and they make apparent the
hidden roots of the discontent, longing and
anger which was later to erupt in the great
movements of women for change.

Fiction/Social History 086358 013 0   256pp
198 × 129 mm paperback

OLD MAIDS

At twenty-five they were 'on the shelf'. But
were they embittered spinsters or independent
women?

The grim image of the 'old maid' as a ridiculous,
pathetic, unlovable, unlovely and unloving
creature has traditionally shadowed young
women. Many have married unhappily, or
submitted to constricting domestic roles, rather
than face its terrors.

Susan Koppelman has discovered and collected
this treasury of 'old maid' stories, written –
often by 'old maids' themselves – between
1835 and 1891 in the USA. With her substantial
introduction as a guide, the reader is taken on
an illuminating excursion into the parlours of the
nineteenth century, as the voices of single
women mark out the gradual shift between
spinsterhood suffered and independence
welcomed.

£4.95   0 86358 014 9

SUFFRAGETTES

A Story of Three Women

by Gertrude Colmore

This is eyewitness fiction – a suffragette novel written in 1911. It is the story of Sally, Edith and Geraldine; three women who, although from different walks of life in early twentieth-century England, find a common cause in the campaign for women's suffrage. They take part in real events which affect their own lives dramatically, and for one of them with tragic consequences.

The story, based on true incidents, is introduced by Dale Spender, who fills in the historical facts and identifies the historical figures behind the fictional narrative and the fictional characters.

Paper £4.95   Fiction 0 86358 041 6   320pp

PLUM BUN

A novel without a moral

by Jessie Redmon Fauset, with an introduction by Deborah E. McDowell

First published in 1929, this novel by an important writer of the Harlem Renaissance chronicles the 'coming of age' of Angela Murray, her development from an adolescent crippled by romantic assumptions about men and marriage, to a woman ready to face the harsh realities of living as a black woman in a racist and sexist culture.

In the introduction to this first British edition, Deborah McDowell shows how Jessie Fauset used the trappings of 'Women's romances' for subversive purposes and challenged the values and assumptions of the middle class.

Paper £4.95   Fiction 0 86358 044 0   396pp